Ibn Al Bitar's Voyages

ALY BRISHA

Ibn Al Bitar's Voyages
Copyright © 2019 by Aly Brisha

All rights reserved. No part of this publication may be reproduced, distributed, or transmitted in any form or by any means, including photocopying, recording, or other electronic or mechanical methods, without the prior written permission of the author, except in the case of brief quotations embodied in critical reviews and certain other non-commercial uses permitted by copyright law.

Tellwell Talent
www.tellwell.ca

ISBN
978-0-2288-1267-8 (Paperback)
978-0-2288-1268-5 (eBook)

Dedicated to the memory of professor Ahmed Abd Allah Rozza,
Leader of the forgotten student revolution
in Tahrir Square (1972).

Special acknowledgment to my trip companion:
My beloved Maha

English Edition Introduction

In January 2011, when Arab people finally demanded their freedom, the sky was the limit. After overthrowing the generals, the creation of a new future seemed possible.

But gradually, dreams became nightmares.

As a journalist specializing in extremism and terrorism, I have worked on fire lines in many locations. I have stared into the eyes of death, while it hovers over the ruins of cities and people and turns those who demand freedom into refugees or the dead.

The more details I gather in the lands of death, the more I realize how military dictatorships and religious extremism are twins feeding on violence and hatred. Both compete for authority, but in the end they are two sides of the same coin.

However, this novel is neither about me nor my journalistic work. It is (to a certain extent) about the lost love message that was buried for eight centuries at the gates of Rome. Hence, here I am sweeping the dust and preaching it among people again.

I would like to thank all who contributed to the translation and preparation of this published version in English, years after it was published in Arabic:

- Creative translator, Manar Adel, who translated the Arabic text into English
- Editor-in-chief, Kurtis Storey, whose enthusiasm made it possible for this novel to be published in English
- Editor of the final version, Jen MacBride, who made the text vivid and the experience more fun and professional by scrutinizing every word and giving me tips on the structure and the flow of events

Thanks to my dear brother, Mohammed Brisha, who was the first one to encourage me to translate my works and who translated my first novel himself. He overcame the challenges that could have made a lazy person like me reluctant to venture forth.

Aly

IN 1258, THE ABBASID CALIPHATE IN BAGHDAD FELL AT THE HANDS OF THE TATARS... AND IT TOOK YEARS BEFORE SULTAN ZAHIR BAYBARS REVIVED THE ABBASID CALIPHATE UNDER THE TUTELAGE OF THE MAMLUK SULTANS IN EGYPT.

ON 29 NOVEMBER 1268, POPE CLEMENT IV DIED, LEAVING THE HOLY SEAT IN ROME EMPTY UNTIL 1 SEPTEMBER 1271. THESE TWO YEARS AND 276 DAYS ARE KNOWN AS THE *GREAT VACANCY*, THE LONGEST PERIOD IN THE HISTORY OF THE CATHOLIC CHURCH SPENT WITHOUT A POPE.

Traveller's Hymn:

"O my bag

My friend

Are you fed up of my trip?

Did you get bored of your alienation?

And mine?"

Prologue

Strange sky... strange faces and throats cheering brutally... Death in exile haunts everyone who joined the journey and sailed the sea, breaking through the western horizon that is pigmented by the bleeding of the sun while taking its last breath in a glorious sunset.

The chaos of the masses is bound by invisible filaments stretching from the prestigious rooted discipline above the wooden platform, which was quickly built only yesterday. The dark robes of the priests. The cross badge on the armour of the knights and soldiers. Their chief is distinguished by the purple badges awarded to him years ago by the pope in a great ceremony, the magnificence of which was narrated everywhere.

There is a horse-drawn carriage carrying a cage... in the cage, the wreck of a man is driven to his inevitable fate. He does not care about the dirt that is thrown at him by the crowds. His past is so full of pain that what he is suffering now is like a walk through a beautiful forest filled with fairies.

He looks through the crowd, searching for his two companions, or even just one of them. His companions partook the journey with him from the east; fought the mythical dragon with him; and shared the secrets and the drugs of the unknown mummy. The shadow of a smile germinates amidst the clotted blood on his face. He does not know whether he is pleased that they survived, or if he misses their presence at the event in which he plays the main role. He listens carefully as if, amidst the roar of the crowd, he can hear a faint sigh of sympathy. It means that at least one of his companions is here.

The iron cage rattles when it hits the iron armour of the soldiers. The door screeches while opening its iron mouth before spitting him into the hands of the torturers. They drag him through the arena to a pile of wood that has been collected by the hands of the believers. The oblivious elderly women donated some of the fuel kept for the winter so that the flames can reach up to the sky… They sacrificed their warmth on stormy nights to approach God with the firewood of Hell.

"Death to the heretic!"

"Morte al eretico!"

"Mortem ad haereticus!"

The cheering of the crowd increases while the solemn court reads the indictment. The soldiers tie him to a pole on top of the wood pile. There is brief silence, as if the crowd is holding its breath to give space for the flame to breathe while being transferred from the soldier's torch to the fuel-soaked straw. Then both the fire and the crowd roar while the flames climb slowly but inexorably up his clothes to completely envelop him in their deadly embrace.

Preface

Alexandria, 3 February 2011

"Last call for the flight to Rome. Passengers, please head quickly to Gate Number One!"

This sentence, repeated by the air hostess in English and Arabic, followed me as I tried to push through the crowds departing from the Alexandria airport. Usually I was keen enough to arrive at the airport two hours prior to the flight. I preferred to be eaten by boredom in the waiting halls rather than being out of breath from having to chase the last call. However, the chaos that inhabited the streets of Alexandria since "The Friday of Anger" had toppled my airport rituals. I arrived only half an hour before the plane took off. The airhostess agreed to board my luggage after she found fifty EGP tucked in my passport.

"Have a happy trip, Mr. Daniel!" she said, smiling.

But the officer in passport control did not smile. He checked my passport, stared at me grouchily, and asked, "What is your religion: Muslim or Christian?"

"It is written there, sir."

"Daniel Mohamed Abdul Razak... Wait off to the side until we check what your religion is: Muslim, Christian, or Christianized[1]. Where the hell did you come from?"

I swallowed my anger at the roughness and ruggedness of the officer. My father gave me three gifts: my name, my profession, and a hot file in state security. I liked only one of my father's gifts. I especially hated the other two whenever I stood in front of an official with a strict grimace and a certain eagle seal.

I reluctantly obeyed the military order, as I did not want to be later than I already was.

Evening talk shows insisted on claiming that the security chaos taking place in Egypt since "The Friday of Anger" was due to people disrespecting the law and wishing to be free from constraints and order.

"Everyone must come together to restore the prestige of the police." The presenter who said this last night was clearly nervous while answering phone calls from people recounting harrowing tales about the horrors they lived in the shadow of lawlessness: some were in tears, some were hysterical. Some of the stories seemed hard to believe.

Two days prior, a young man had stated that he was from Alexandria, living on a street near my house in the Sidi Bishr district, close to the Church of the Saints. He said that the church was being attacked by bearded youth throwing stones at it. I immediately went down to the street in question and, lo and behold, it was quiet. Just to make sure, I walked to the church and found that no one was attacking it. The effects of the bombing, which killed dozens of people at the beginning of the year, are still engraved in the walls of the church and the surrounding buildings. However, there *were* bearded men that night as mentioned on television.

---

[1] To be Christianized means to be a Muslim who has converted to Christianity. In Egypt and many other Islamic countries, this is a crime. In some countries, this is a crime punishable by death.

The officer told me to wait, so I did. Minutes later, I was chased again by the last call to board the plane leaving for Rome. I put on a mask, decorated with a fake smile, as I walked slowly towards the officer. I told him the old story that I had invented long ago for whenever I faced a problem because of my name. This story, in an unfamiliar way, combines two religious identities.

"My father was one of the hero soldiers who fought in the October War. I was born after he returned victorious from the battlefront, so he insisted on naming me after his Christian friend, Daniel. Daniel was shot by an Israeli soldier as he was protecting my father during the crossing of the Bar Lev Line."

These frequent experiences taught me that this story hits home quickly with many people, particularly those who work for the government. I used to emphasize certain words such as *Bar Lev Line* and *The October War*, as they gave the story a magical effect by adding a tinge of nostalgia mixed with pride.

Minutes later, I was climbing the stairs of the plane. The airhostess gave me a hasty smile for show, barely masking the blame while almost pushing me into my seat. I think I noticed her later, after the plane took off, breathing a sigh of relief. It was as if she had been standing in a minefield, expecting something to explode at any moment under her feet.

When she came around later during turbulence to make sure that all seat belts were fastened, she told me in English, tinged with an Italian accent, that takeoff had been delayed twice before for various reasons and that the crew had had to spend the night in the military lounge connected to the airport. Officials had refused to transfer the crew to one of Alexandria's hotels out of fear of the deteriorating security situation that prevailed in the city's streets — this despite the curfew. I looked outside the window of the plane, trying to find, within the streets of Alexandria, the rivers of human bodies in demonstration: its crowds flooding everywhere and gathering in various public squares, a rumbling sea facing the Corniche at Al Qae'ed Ibrahim Mosque. If my father were still alive, he would have filled these squares with the enthusiastic sound of his voice. He would have travelled back in time forty years to become a young man again among today's youth, chewing stony cake[2] and shedding tears as usual while he read poetry by Amal Dunqul:

> *The soldiers came: a circle of shields and war helmets*
> *Slowly, slowly drawing closer*
> *From every direction*
> *And the singers in the stone cake clenched*
> *And released*
> *Like a heartbeat*
> *Their throats aflame*
> *To warm them against the cold and the biting darkness*
> *They raised their anthems in the face of the approaching guards*

Alexandria disappeared behind the horizon, snuffed out by the whiteness of the clouds and the blueness of the sea. I returned to my small bag and opened it, trying to recall the mysterious lines that drew me far away from Egypt in its critical moment to take me to naughty old Rome with its renewed childishness. Ibn Al Bitar calls me from behind the clouds, the lines of his prose written in ornate Italian. He ends with an official seal and a solemn, majestic signature.

---

[2] The stony cake is a famous poem by the Egyptian poet Amal Dunqul, written to tell the story of the demonstrations of Cairo University students in Tahrir Square which were brutally suppressed in January 1972.

The Second Voyage

Homs, July 1259

Human Senses could not miss the colour, sound, or smell of extermination. Knights of Tatars were spreading celebratory death in their own way, performing their black mission with much joy. Murder, arson, and rape were met with the haunting sounds of bereavement mixed in with the sharply contrasting shouts of victory. Some of the soldiers slowed down in front of a dying woman; they shared a laugh before one of them shoves his dagger into her stomach to bring out a fetus writhing like a flayed snake. One soldier removed the blood from the baby's body and screamed ecstatically that he had won the bet. Another soldier exhaled in ire and took from his clothes a golden ring retaining the remnants of the human finger that accompanied its owner during his lifetime. The soldier had grabbed the finger with the ring so as not to waste time while collecting his spoils. Now, he presented it without sorrow as a price for a quick bet. A quick loss did not matter since the city was full of fingers and necks dressed in gold, waiting for brutal daggers to harvest them.

Before the Tatars entered the city, Najm El Din Ibn Al Bitar had left it. The daylight trip the family made on Sheikh Yusuf's meagre donkey did not prevent him, whenever he looked back, to see smoke rising from the site of the city that lay at the horizon. His eye could not miss the flock of vultures gathered either, waiting for a banquet of human corpses. Details of the horrific massacres preceded the lean donkey to the next village where the exhausted family rested. Al Ashraf Musa Bin Sherkoh, the owner of Homs (from 1246 to 1263), opened the doors of the fortified citadel to the armies of the Tatars. He received the leader, Katbugha Noyan, at the door of the castle, slaughtered some sacrifices, and left the Tatar soldiers to practice the conquest's victory rituals in the city. They had the right to do so for three days; the soldiers would then be satisfied enough with the blood and their spoils.

Ibn Al Bitar looked behind him once more. His blue eyes met his mother's which were bobbing in tandem with the donkey's movements. Pain and tears were in all four eyes. He was only ten years old, which did not give him enough experience to deal with the tragedy of homelessness, the trauma of leaving the walls of the warm house, the faces of good neighbours, the familiar streets and markets, to go out into the wide-open horizon in which the unknown creatures wandered. There was no difference between humans, trees, animals, and supernatural creatures that inhabit the tales of grandmothers.

By midday, he needed to urinate but Sheikh Yusuf grumbled in discontent, as they were not to waste a single moment on their journey. They were, after all, walking through an open valley. Once the Knights of the Tatars finished their conquest rituals in Homs, they would comb the surrounding countryside in search of more spoils and human sacrifices.

They were obliged however to stop shortly after that. Sheikh Yusuf became more flexible when Mariam was in agony. He allowed her to have a short rest under the shade of a lush tree. Ibn Al Bitar took advantage of this time to empty his bladder and to fill his canteen from a nearby stream. He then rushed to his exhausted mother sitting under the tree to give her water. The moment of relaxation passed quickly before the family gathered up their things to continue their journey and join the droves of people wandering in search of safety, far away from the Tatars' swords.

Refugees gathered together in the evening in the outskirts of the next village to share legends that were fueled by horror and panic. Tatar soldiers were not like other humans. They could ride a horse for three consecutive nights without resting or eating. It was enough for a Tatar soldier to cut his forearm with his dagger and suck blood from his wound. From this wound, he would receive enough sustenance to keep him going for days.

One of the exhausted fleeing elderly refugees nodded his head silently, confirming the anecdotes[3]:

"They are not human beings. They are the people of Gog and Magog. The dam, which was built by Zulqarnain to separate them from other nations, collapsed. Because of this, they became an overwhelming torrent sweeping the country and knocking on the doors of the Resurrection. The end of the world is approaching. There hasn't been a caliphate in the land of the Muslims since Baghdad was destroyed, and Caliph Musta'sim was killed in the most heinous style. For the first time since the cessation of the divine revelation, there is no caliphate, and no one to reign except Jesus, God's Messenger, Son of Mary; who will descend from the sky to defend Islam.[4] Believers will then gather around him and he will fight to kill the Antichrist and make justice prevail."

No one was listening, but the old refugee did not care. In fact, the talk of the old man was received somewhat hesitantly in the minds of each refugee. The eyes that had stared at death a little while ago would become more capable of perceiving gloom in the coming days.

---

[3] This section contains quotations from Islamic mythology related to the Apocalypse.

[4] In Islamic mythology, Christ returns to the world at the end of time to help Muslims to the final triumph.

The old man shook his head – which a Tatar would cut off tomorrow – and swore that he saw with his own eyes the great Katbugha Noyan when he entered Homs Castle. He was a good-looking leader, who sometimes hooked his long, braided beard behind his ear. Dominant and imposing, he entered the mosque and climbed the rostrum to see the castle. He then came out of the western door, entered a wrecked shop, and urinated while people watched. When he had finished, some of his companions wiped him only once with some cotton. Katbugha did not look anything like the anecdotes about the Antichrist. He was not one-eyed and the word "liar" did not appear on his forehead. It could be Hulagu, his master. Or maybe the Antichrist was still waiting impatiently in a faraway land, anticipating that the people of Gog and Magog would pave the world for him, to attack, torture, and murder the believers.

Interestingly, Katbugha Noyan was Christian, and not a heathen like the rest of the Tatars. However, he followed the Nestorian doctrine, and it was said that he tried to become an ally of the coastal princes of the Crusaders to fight the Egyptian Sultan, but they refused. His nephew, who was a messenger between the Tatars and the coastal princes, was killed by the Crusader Prince of Sidon.

Ibn Al Bitar's blue eyes took in the faces of the refugees. This night was not pitch-black, as the shining stars illuminated the summer sky despite the absence of a moon. Talks about the end of the world were not new for Ibn Al Bitar. During the last years, there had been recurrent stories about a fire lasting for a month erupting in Al Hejaz Land, at the east of the Madina El Monawara at Shaza Valley opposite to Uhud Mountain. The fire had spread, engulfing the valley in flames. Sparks had flown out of the mountain, melting rock and decimating the entire city.

A few days ago, before the Tartars invaded the city, the sheikh of the big mosque in Homs narrated what had happened; he advised people to repent: "A huge fire spouted out at Shaza Valley over twelve miles long, four miles wide, and nine feet deep. Rocks were liquefied and turned into black coal. The homes of Medina used this fire for illumination until every house had a lamp. The people in Mecca saw the light of the fire, thus the people of Medina sought refuge in the tomb of the Prophet Mohamed. They prayed, asking God for forgiveness; released their slaves; and gave offerings. The fire was bright. One of the Bedouins, who was in the town of Basra in the land of Sham, mentioned that through the darkness they could clearly see their camels. On Friday night, at the beginning of the holy month of Ramadan, a huge fire erupted at the Prophet's mosque in Medina after a piece of coal fell out of a lamp. Many rows and even some pillars were gone, and the ceiling of the holy room was burned."

The sheikh of the big mosque of Homs then raised his voice, yelling so loud that the veins of his neck seemed about to burst: "Repent to God; doomsday is coming soon."

Ibn Al Bitar snuck out of the speech, which had evolved by then into a soliloquy about the end of the world.

He went to his mother who was fighting death. The trip had increased the intensity of her disease, which she faced with a weak eagerness. It was her destiny not to reach safety, and so she wished to die as soon as possible so as not to delay him from reaching his destination in a safe land.

His blue eyes sparkled with tears. He hugged her; she smiled and unlocked her safe full of ancient secrets.

"We came from Egypt and you will go back there."

She searched through her pockets and brought out a ring capped with a carving of a wondrous mythical animal with two heads breathing fire.

"One day, you will need this ring as evidence of your lineage, so that you can get the inheritance of your father, whom you did not get to see even once."

Her weak voice poured all the old secrets in his ears. Astonished, he listened. At this moment, his life was changed forever. He now had to embark on a long voyage.

"IT WAS AGREED THAT TWELVE OF THE MARINE MAMLUKS PASSED BY THE ISRAELIS. THEY STAYED THERE FOR FIVE DAYS, CONFUSED. ON THE SIXTH DAY, THEY SAW BLACKNESS ON THE HORIZON, SO THEY APPROACHED IT. IT WAS A GREAT CITY WITH FORTIFIED WALLS AND DOORS ALL MADE OF GREEN MARBLE."

TAQEY EL DIN AL MAQRIZI (1378)

The First Voyage

Damietta, 1249

Najm El Din Ibn Al Bitar talked to me thusly about his first journey:

> I was destined to start my journeys in this world prior to my birth. In my mother's womb, I did not feel the effects of travelling and the sadness of the scenes that unfolded. Covered by the darkness of the night, my mother went out of her small village within the boundaries of Faraskur near Damietta at the mouth of the River Nile.
>
> On her way towards the unknown, she had no companion other than Yusuf, the stableman. At that time, Yusuf worked in the palace of Prince Fakhr El Din, the commander of the army of El Saleh Najm El Din Ayoub. Yusuf had a scrawny donkey which was one of the livestock left behind after the Frank Army was defeated.
>
> The Franks had ruled Damietta for ten months. They took it without war, right after their ship landed on its shores. My mother remembers the day they

arrived, which changed her life. It was Friday the 21st of Safar in the Islamic Calendar. The ship was carrying a large number of soldiers led by their great King Louis, son of Louis.

I barely heard my mother's voice while she explained to me the title of their commander. Roi de France was the title in the Frank language. All the Franks on the coast joined them, attacking Damietta in one mighty wave.

"Do you speak French, Mother?"

She smiled in spite of the atonality.

"I learned some during the several months I spent in their camp. After their soldiers kidnapped me, they took me to one of their leaders: Peter or Pitar, I am not sure. I found out later that he was the brother of the King of the Franks."

For three days, my mother turned him down as he patiently courted her. On the fourth night, it happened. Modesty prevented me from asking for details and shame stopped her from sharing, but she swore to me that this did not take place until Prince Pitar officially married her. He brought his brother, the king, to her room to witness his marriage to the beautiful captive. It seemed like the king did not welcome this whim so he allowed the high priest of Jerusalem to lead the marriage rituals.

My mother breathed with difficulty while trying to fight her exhaustion from travelling. Meanwhile, the death birds were flying over Homs which was attacked by the swords of the Tatars.

"The high priest of Jerusalem joined the Frank Army with his cross and his sword. I did not understand the gibberish of the marriage rituals but it all ended when Prince Pitar put his ring onto my finger."

I gazed at the ring, which my mother had put into my hand a few hours prior to her death. I recalled her narrating my first trip when I was just starting to form in her womb.

"When the Franks were defeated in Faraskur by the Egyptian soldiers and their King Turan Shah, armies invaded the camp of the King and the princes. The King was captured while Prince Pitar and the remnants of the army retreated to Damietta. I wandered around during this chaos. Soldiers attacked the Frank people and they busied themselves for some time collecting the loot and plunder. As for me, I was destined to be a captive either to the Franks or the Mamluks. So, I went out to the vast fields hiding under the papyrus jungles. My village was a few miles away, but I was afraid to go back to my family since I was pregnant. Should I tell them that I did not yield and show them the ring? No, no one would believe me. And even if they did believe me, who would have mercy? And if they had mercy who would forgive? Only God the Merciful and Forgiving knows that I did not let go of my honour and religion. I was a captive and had to choose between being raped or accepting an unlawful marriage."

Tears sparkled in my mother's eyes as she searched mine for pity. But she only found the pain of a child crying for his mother. She gently hugged me and called for Sheikh Yusuf. I caught a glimpse of his face

covered in tears. I had never seen him cry like this. Like the rocks of Mount Sinai, his eyes needed the stick of God's prophet Moses to spout water. Prophet Moses disappeared, Mariam was still breathing, and the man of stone collapsed beside her. At first sight I could not tell who was the crying child and who was the dignified sheikh.

. . . . .

All of a sudden, the air hostess interrupted Ibn Al Bitar. She then raised her voice to confirm the necessity of tightening the seat belt. She asked the passenger next to me to straighten his seat and he obeyed. Landing started and the lights of Rome appeared. The night clouds revealed a nebula of eternal light wrestling within the space. The Lady of the Old World was still sparkling with its special charm, linking the sky and the earth. Rome was sacred by the sway of Roman swords, papal crosses, Bernini marble, and Michelangelo's art. Before leaving the constantly crowded airport, I was hit by the aroma of cappuccino wafting out of one of the takeaway cafés frequently visited by the passengers.

There was no need for me to stand in a long queue for the baggage pick-up. Long ago, I adopted habits for quick travelling. My carry-on bag was enough. It carried all the necessary things; it was my alternative home. I carried it with me whenever I was away from my country. I carried my long wool coat on my arm, my survival tool for all weather. My own history and the geography of my trips were summed up by what I now carried on my shoulder and arm while walking slowly and enjoying the smell of cappuccino and delicious pasta. Usually, I did not eat airport meals. However, in Rome, which gave everything a part of its soul, I made an exception. Food in Rome was not a means to live; it was life itself. I spent almost half an hour enjoying the fettuccini pasta covered in white sauce and chunks of seafood accompanied by a cappuccino.

When I was about to exit the gate, the other passengers who were on the same flight were just finished picking up their luggage. A young man with eastern facial features stood by the gate, carrying a sign with my name written on it. It was spelled the way I am used to seeing it in foreign languages: *Professor Danny Razak*.

As I came closer to him, he welcomed me in a Moroccan accent with an enthusiasm that delivered warmth through February's cold weather. He told me he was from Tunisia, and he talked eagerly about what was happening in Egypt.

"Soon the oppression will be gone, and the nightmare will come to an end. Egypt will join Tunisia on their way to freedom very soon, God willing. We waited so long for this moment, Professor, so long."

He said this with a smile. His words were reminiscent of something being repeated on one of the news channels, so I smiled. I could not cope with his enthusiasm. I was embarrassed that he was praising the Egyptian revolution, which I had watched exactly like him — through the television. I answered his consecutive questions with short replies, avoiding the enthusiasm and being cautious not to express a specific opinion.

In the lobby of the hotel, the receptionist told me that the academy's car would pick me up at 10:00 a.m. I went to my room feeling exhausted. I put my bag in the closet then searched for the direction of the Kaaba. Once situated, I quickly washed up and prayed a shortened prayer; I then lay down on the bed impatiently. Tiredness would not prevent me from calling Ibn Al Bitar to continue his story for me. It was not appropriate for him to leave me stuck in his First Voyage.

. . . . .

In the darkness of the unknown, I passed miles of desert stretching in different directions. Hoofprints in the sand drew the lines of my first trip. I lived in my mother's womb, between her hope and her despair.

One moment she felt so weak that she asked God to forget her. She even asked to have a miscarriage. The night she escaped from the French camp, she was lost in the fields of Faraskour but she didn't dare walk the miles that would take her to her village and people. Yusuf the stableman appeared from the darkness; he was one of the people of her village who had been captured the same night she was taken. It was only because he was also a clever veterinarian that he didn't face what the other captives faced; the Franks killed men but they did not kill the livestock or the veterinarians. Their knights needed those who could look after the horses and other livestock.

The two homeless had known each other in the past and carried a common shame. Going back to their village meat shame to Mariam and embarrassment for Yusuf. No one would forget that she became pregnant by the Franks nor that he served them, even though it was against their will.

The two homeless turned eastward. A weak donkey escaping from the Frank camp was their ride. Mariam rode the donkey since she was pregnant; Sheikh Yusuf walked ahead by a few paces. After two days, the green valley disappeared and the dreariness of the desert welcomed them. During the day, the sun was hanging in the sky heating the transient over the sand. At night, the stars were like angry eyes watching over them. Day was torment and night was jeopardy; the travellers fluctuated between these two miseries. They were two, and their third companion was the fetus. Or they were three, and their fourth companion was the donkey. This wouldn't matter, because they were all about to die.

On the sixth day, they saw on the horizon something black which they headed towards. It was a great city with high walls and fortified doors all made of green marble, not inhabited by any bird or human being. They wandered down the empty, majestic streets; the market and homes were covered in sand and whenever they touched anything, it would disintegrate. But they found nine dinars,[5] inscribed with the image of a deer encircled with writing in Hebrew. They dug through the earth and extracted a slab. They lifted it; it was a tank of water cooler than ice. They drank and took some for later, then they continued their trip all night.

They eventually ran into a convoy of Bedouins. They asked for help. The Bedouins accepted and took them to Kark Fort. There, they offered the dinars to money-changers; some of them said that these dinars were made in the age of Moses.

They asked about the Green City and they were told that it had been built when Israelis were there. Sometimes it was flooded in sand; sometimes it was not. Only a lost person could find it. They exchanged each dinar for one hundred dirhams[6].

---

[5] Dinar: golden coin used in many ancient states in the East.

[6] Dirham: silver coin.

This is Rome

Rome, 4 February 2011

Somewhere between light and darkness, a monotonous and provocative ringing emerged. I ignored it but it kept ringing. I barely opened my eyes. The features of hotel rooms are alike; I no longer knew in which foreign country I was waking up. Bit by bit I started to regain my senses through the fog that separated sleep from wakefulness. My watch said it was 10:30 a.m., but the light of the early morning that penetrated the curtains indicated that my watch was lying. Gradually, I recalled the time and place. I had not adjusted my watch to Rome time yet; it was still Alexandria's time that dictated the rhythm of my body. The ringing persisted, so I had to pick up the phone.

Through the phone came a feminine voice speaking English in a cheerful Italian accent:

"Professor Razak. Welcome to Rome!"

A moment of silence.

"I apologize for waking you up early. This is Maria Satriano, your personal assistant during your stay."

I remembered the email I had printed. That name was mentioned in it. The pages were spread over and under the bed as I had fallen asleep while reading.

She repeated her apology then told me that she would be waiting for me in an hour in the lobby.

"Would that be fine with you?"

"Yes, thank you," I replied.

My own personal assistant! I wondered what she looked like. Her family name indicated a southern Italian origin. I was willing to bet that she would not be blonde. Most likely she would have silky black hair and a thin face with a long nose.

Most Italian women were not so beautiful, but some could be attractive and vivid; their voices rhythmic and with the soul of the Mediterranean Sea flowing inside them.

"Women, coffee, and wine. Italy makes this trio different and distinctive. Only those who have fine taste are aware of that." My father used to say that, smiling, when talking about my British wife whom he always described as cold.

"Sophia Loren, for example, has a big mouth and an inconsistent nose. Her beauty might be considered below average. But her attractive and vivid soul puts her on the throne of beauty," he would always say.

I ended the call and cautiously removed the blanket to avoid sending the rest of the papers to the floor. I collected them carefully and put the officially signed paper at the very beginning. Then I began to get ready.

The delicate curtains filtered a glowing sun which was unusual for Rome in February. It felt like the warm weather in Alexandria, with the refreshing smell of rain. It had not rained much in Alexandria that winter.

The demonstrations of January 25 took place at the height of winter and any rainstorm could have dispersed the protesters and brought them home. But God wanted the weather to remain warm and sunny for the last few days.

"Miracle, it is simply a miracle," so many of the demonstrators said, chasing the divine signs in their actions.

I overheard some young guys considering this divine miracle. Some of the Imams noted this miracle in the last Friday prayer speech:

"The Friday of Anger[7] was on the second day of El Karm storm, when rains are heaviest in Alexandria and usually lasting for six days. If the storm hits the city as usual, Alexandria will not be in headlines. Protesters would not be able to be on the streets on the Friday of Anger and the streets would not be warm for the protestors at the square of Mahatet El Raml and around El Qae'ed Ibrahim Mosque. The light rain was cool and peaceful upon the millions of angry and rebelling protestors. It flourishes and does not hurt; it washes the heart without chilling to the bone. The seasonal storm is generous to the Egyptians."

The Suez government had the first strike in the Egyptian uprising against the Mubarak regime, but Alexandria had the final say. On the Day of Anger, the government had almost no authority in the de facto second capital. There was a joke among the protestors that if Mubarak did not leave, they could easily declare Alexandria an independent city.

These thoughts came to mind as I prepared to pray. Sometimes I had no time to pray, but I was always keen to wash up with cold water. It was a habit I learned from my Nanny Attiyat years ago.

As usual, I did not bring a lot of clothes with me so as not to get confused when choosing what to wear. The black wool trousers and the pullover with the high neck gave me a comfortable, yet semi-formal appearance which helped me navigate both academic and practical worlds. The heavy grey coat helped me to bear the

---

[7] The Friday of Anger was on the 28th of January, 2011. It was the third day of the Egyptian revolution against Mubarak, in which there were large and bloody confrontations between millions of demonstrators and police forces in most Egyptian cities. The revolution ended with the control of the demonstrators on the main squares in the cities after the fall of about eight hundred dead and the announcement of an open strike until Mubarak stepped down.

continual weather fluctuations in various European capitals; it was on my arm during good weather and became a part of my body when I was shivering. I needed no more clothes.

Half an hour later, as I was crossing the lobby to the front door, I heard the soft Italian accent calling my name:

"Professor Razak?"

An Asian woman in her mid-twenties approached me enthusiastically.

"I did not expect you to finish your breakfast in less than half an hour. I am Maria Satriano."

I was shocked by the fact that I had lost a bet with myself. She was neither blonde nor brunette; she looked Japanese. She was vivid and beautiful, and her voice was not devoid of the usual music. But she did not look like any Italian woman I had ever known or expected to know.

"Thank you, Signorina Satriano. Actually, I did not have breakfast yet. I thought you would be here in half an hour and that I would have time to have breakfast Italian-style, far from the food court inside the hotel."

"Great idea! Cappuccino e Cornetto is a great place, only a few steps away from the hotel."

The cornetto is the Italian equivalent of a French croissant. Most Italians are not aware that the most popular breakfast in their country carries an Arabic origin. The word *cornetto* is the Italian pronunciation of the Arabic word *qarn,* which means horn. The croissant is called cornetto because it looks like the horn of an ox. As for the delicious Italian *mocha* coffee, it is a twist on the name of the ancient Yemeni harbour *Mukha,* through which coffee used to be imported to Europe by Italian merchants.

Maria did not wait for me to reply, instead instantly moving forward. I followed her outside. The weather was colder than I had expected. The rays of the winter sun were poking through heavy clouds.

The usual bustle of Rome carries a unique combination of small cars, motorcycle engines, and human voices speaking quick Italian. Large cities usually wake up in a hustle while the ancient, prestigious ones give the waking moments an aura of dignity and aristocratic elegance. This is how it is in Alexandria, which receives every morning as if lighting a new candle of immortality.

A few steps outside the hotel, we were hit by the fragrance of fresh baking mixed with a strong aroma of coffee. Busy bees seemed to have invaded the streets, some of which were crowded in front of a small, full shop. In the early morning, most people had their breakfast standing in the inside bar, taking quick sips from their cup of espresso and biting into their delicious cornetto. But customers that came a little later were slower, sitting on the small tables scattered inside, enjoying their breakfast without looking at their watch every three minutes. Maria chose a small table beside a huge glass window. She insisted that she would bring the breakfast out to the table herself.

"They serve macchiato in this shop. What do you say?"

"Thank you, but I prefer a cappuccino. I would also like a chocolate cornetto, please."

Moving quickly yet gracefully, she went to place the order. When she came back, she found me behind the papers about Ibn Al Bitar with which I had stayed up late last night.

"In Rome, do the same as Romans do. Romans never mix work with breakfast," she said.

I helped her to put the plates and cups down. She sat opposite me and started talking enthusiastically.

"I am honoured to work with you, Professor Razak. My colleagues at the university envy me for this assignment.

Everyone is interested in your latest discoveries in the Siwa Oasis. Your publication in which you blend history with literature is my favourite. I feel that you are writing history as if you were an eyewitness, without using the dull language we are used to in academic studies."

"Are you still a student?"

"I graduated two years ago from La Sapienza University. I am now working on my Masters. In a few months, I would love you to honour me by attending my thesis defence. Professor Geovany is the one who supervises this research, and he is the one who nominated me to be your personal assistant."

Professor Roberto Geovany was the president of the Romanian Academy for Monuments. He owned the prestigious signature on that official paper which brought me here. I found myself complimenting her.

"I am thankful to Professor Roberto for making an excellent choice."

To this, she replied with a great cheerfulness: "I hope I can meet your expectations."

I tried to change the subject back to Ibn Al Bitar.

"Tell me about this archaeological dig. How did it happen and what are the latest updates?"

Trying to contain the situation, the Egyptian government had cut off most internet communication since the Friday of Anger. Maria had not been able to send me either the tickets or photocopies of the manuscripts which weren't found until yesterday.

"So far, the details of this archaeological discovery have not been announced. Professor Geovany considers it one of the most important discoveries of the twenty-first century. Coincidence played an important role in exploring the cache in which these manuscripts were buried, which was in an abandoned field outside the borders of Rome."

"Yes, but what about the Demotic manuscripts which were found. Have their era been confirmed?"

"The cache consisted of two pottery jars with papyrus manuscripts inside them. It was strange from the very first moment they way that some of the manuscripts were written: some with the Arabic script and others with the Demotic. Surprisingly, laboratory tests on the papyrus revealed that they were made in the thirteenth-century AD. We did some radiocarbon tests in the past few days to confirm that these manuscripts date back to sometime between 1260 and 1290 AD."

"That's incredible!"

"It is! The archaeological value of this discovery is priceless and will impact historical and archaeological studies, as it inevitably proves that the ancient Egyptian language has been used more recently than expected. All the researchers and archaeologists had the idea that the fourth- or the fifth-century AD was the end of the old Egyptian language and of Pharaonic civilization, which vanished completely after this time; especially since Christianity won the battle over the ancient Pharaonic gods. The Egyptians considered the Pharaonic language and monuments as the legacy for a civilization that was far from the true faith. The Coptic language got some of its features from the ancient Pharaonic language, and some researchers consider it to be a subsidiary of the Pharaonic language. But the Coptic language used Greek letters which differentiated it from the old Egyptian one. That's why the emergence of archaeological evidence that proves that the Demotic script was used in the thirteenth century is considered a revolutionary inversion in archeology: all the more that it was found in in Italy, not in Egypt."

I could not prevent myself from smiling as Maria talked, waving her hands enthusiastically as Italians do. This discovery was as strange as the fact that I was in Rome with a Japanese-looking woman who had a pure Italian name, and who was speaking English in a clear Italian accent.

It seems that my smile and staring stopped her. She smiled back coyly.

"Professor Danny, you seem absent-minded."

I felt those witty eyes penetrate my thoughts. I got confused. I realized that she had caught me observing her features, searching for traditional traits of the Mediterranean people. I had to ask the question I had been wondering since I met her. With an embarrassed smile, I asked, "Well... I mean... I do not know... are you... where are you from?"

The smile on her face evolved into a loud Italian laugh.

"At last!" she said, rather loudly.

Her laugh made me feel even more embarrassed, which in turn made her laugh even more. She called over the waiter and ordered two glasses of orange juice through her bouts of laughter, and then she looked at me.

"Usually people ask me this question when they first meet me. I was sure that you would do that. I was a little bit disappointed when I saw the question in your eyes, but you did not ask."

I hid my confusion by smiling at her and jokingly said, "I am wondering who lost the bet, you or yourself? Anyway, allow me to pay for the orange juice and consider both of you as winners."

"Thank you," she graciously accepted. Then she started talking in a serious manner, "My paternal grandmother was from a Japanese family living in America early in the twentieth century. You know what happened to the Japanese in America when the Second World War began: over a hundred thousand were arrested and sent to camps. It was a human tragedy, forgotten throughout history. My grandmother was one of those forced into such a camp. My grandfather was an Italian merchant stuck in America during the war. You can imagine an Italian man and Japanese woman in a country fighting a fierce war against their own countries. They fell in love, perhaps bonding through this joint oppression. After the war, they moved to Italy. I inherited my grandmother's Asian features, a full embodiment of Mendel's theory of inheritance."

"A white cat with a yellow one... what are the possibilities that one of the third generation would be totally yellow?"

"One-sixteenth, a very low probability but a possible one. I am living proof of that."

"You are speaking Italian with a Southern accent, right?" I asked.

"Oh, I forgot that I am talking with a professor who specializes in linguistics!"

"I specialize in dead languages, not living ones. But I understand Italian pretty well even if I only speak it a little."

"I can see that. Yes, my father's family comes from a rural region near Barry. Maybe the reason that I love archeology is that I worked for a long time at the site of the ancient city of Pompeii. I consider it one of the most spectacular archaeological sites in the world."

Interrupted by ringing, she removed her phone from her bag; and after a short call she stood up.

"Professor Roberto Geovany will be waiting for you in half an hour. We have to move right now!"

I looked at my watch. I did not feel that more than hour and a half had passed. Perhaps it was because I hadn't experienced such a close familiarity that I felt with my personal assistant, who I had met only ninety minutes ago, for many years.

. . . . .

Professor Geovany was very welcoming. The old aristocratic man had been nominated President of UNESCO. Yet every time I met with him, I felt as if he were a simple Alexandrian fisherman sitting in a coffee shop in one of the city's local fisherman districts, El Anfoushi. He shook my hand as if he were clapping it, just as the Alexandrians do. He hugged me and kissed my cheeks on both sides. Again, just like Egyptians do.

He left his comfortable-looking desk to sit with me in a small salon attached to his office. Professor Geovany, along with my father, had a long history of doing excavations in Alexandria. He spoke Arabic in a way that reminded me of how the Greeks used to — the ones that lived in my country dozens of years ago.

Professor Geovany started by asking me about Egypt, how everything was going, and about the progress of the demonstrations. He told me that he was sure that the Egyptians would vanquish the tyranny, and that the oppressive ruler would fall. He was sincere, speaking with real feelings and warmth; but I answered sparingly, as I was in a hurry to start talking about the details of my upcoming mission.

The familiarity soon faded away and, in a serious tone, he emphasized the secrecy of this discovery. The academy wanted to choose the most suitable timing to announce the results after a complete investigation of the cache, the restoration of the documents, and their translation. I stopped him when he mentioned needing to restore the manuscripts, asking him about their condition.

"Unfortunately, some of the papyrus scrolls were badly damaged. The clay pots would have been saved in perfect condition; with the exception of one which was broken during the digging, and water slipped into it. In any case, as you are no doubt aware, we need your cooperation in translating and compiling the text."

Professor Geovany went to his desk and got out some photos of the archaeological site. He explained to me some of the details related to the documentation of excavation happening in adjacent areas. I noticed a photo of a black, irregularly-shaped object. I asked him about it.

"That is part of the mystery of the cache. We realized that it is a bag made of gazelle hide. There was another bag inside made of an unknown, thin leathery material. What is even stranger is that the black material inside it does not look like anything else. It looks like dust but has a greasy feel. Initial analysis confirmed that it is an organic substance, mixed with minerals and other elements that are being separated now for more detailed analysis. We also sent samples for radiocarbon dating. I expect the results will enlighten us about all the mystery that surrounds pretty much everything about this cache."

"What about the Demotic manuscripts? What condition did you find them in, and have you translated any of them?"

"These manuscripts are badly damaged, and unfortunately we have no experts in Demotic writing. As you know, it is the most difficult and rarest style of the old Egyptian writing. While thousands of archaeologists specialize in hieroglyphic writing, only a few can deal with Demotic writing."

I wondered if perhaps that was why I was famous, and that this was the secret behind my continuous travelling among the continents. Thanks to my father, I was able to read and write in Demotic even before I finished primary school. I grew up with these mysterious signs. They were among my earliest childhood memories, to the extent that I do not even remember when I started learning it. Maybe I learned it before I could even write in my mother tongue. Today, according to UNESCO, I am one of the top ten experts in ancient Demotic writing.

"Come on, Professor Geovany! It is not possible that you could not find anyone that could give you any hint about what is written in the manuscripts, even with an initial inaccurate translation. What are you hiding from me?" I asked, smiling.

Professor Geovany laughed and looked at me, saying, "Do not rush, Danny. Maybe I need to know your opinion objectively, free from the opinions of the other academic professors who have already checked the manuscripts."

Professor Geovany continued with a stern warning, "The research team working with us assumed that these were magical writings. Maybe it was part of a mysterious ritual that took place in the thirteenth century that recalled an unknown ethnic power by using an obsolete language. This ritual was prevalent in the Middle Ages and probably one of the reasons for the Inquisition, which was held around the same time these manuscripts were written."

Professor Geovany used the Latin term for the Inquisition, *Inquisitio Haereticae Pravitatis*, which literally means *Investigation of the Heretical Heresies*. My body trembled upon hearing that horrifying term, which reflected an era of great repression, horrible torture, and terrible intimidation experienced in Europe in the period between its historical indolence and the beginning of civilization in the modern era.

My meeting with Professor Geovany took about half an hour, at the end of which he invited me for dinner at his place.

"I will send a car to the hotel to pick you up. Kiara prepared Sayadieh Samak. She thought, with it being the traditional fish plate of Alexandria, it would make you feel like you hadn't left home."

He laughed and winked while saying that. I asked him to send my greetings to his wife. My father used to consider her the best chef who ever lived.

I left the office of Professor Geovany to find Maria waiting for me. She took me to meet the team. I knew most of the Italian academic archaeologists and they knew me as well. Their hospitality complemented their warm feelings towards what was happening in Egypt. Usually Europeans were conservative when talking about Middle Eastern politics, especially as it was well-known that I was not eager to talk about political issues. But there was excitement and enthusiasm among the Italian team members who started asking me about what was taking place in Alexandria, the demonstrations, and Tahrir Square. I could not remain conservative, which I usually do when people start talking politics, and so I showed — probably for the first time since The Friday of Anger — clear sympathy with the demonstrators. I even caught myself for the first time using the term *revolution* to describe the demonstrators.

Strangely, the only team member whom I had not met before, and who was not interested in what was happening in Egypt, was Professor Abd El Hussein El Jaafary, the Iraqi scientist who specialized in investigating the Arabic manuscripts and supervising the renovation. I did not know why he was so cautious towards me. He was a dignified old man with a white beard and black eyes that popped out repulsively.

He raised his veined hand to shake mine, while saying in an arrogant manner, "Welcome, son."

Perhaps it was the age difference that made him maintain a distance with me. The way he treated me reminded me of the way I was treated by the professors at University of Alexandria: your position was set by your age and seniority bypassed efficiency, similar to any old bureaucratic system. Some professors considered me the pampered kid who inherited a position he didn't deserve, who felt proud of his degree from Cambridge University. Egyptian universities were part of a country that was ruled by authorities as old as the government itself. The media described the Prime Minister as a *young man* only because he was not yet sixty years old. It was normal for me, then, to be treated by the university professors as a kid, even when I became one of the most important world experts in Demotic writing before I hit my thirties.

The previous dean of Alexandria University never forgave me for getting a PhD scholarship in London against his wishes. Just one call from State Security resolved the issue and tore down all obstacles the dean put up to prevent me from getting the scholarship. This call cost me a lot but it made me fly away from Egypt at a critical moment of personal suffering.

The first meeting with the team was full of warmth. I was eager to see the Demotic manuscripts. I asked Maria about it. She said that unlike the Arabic manuscripts, the Demotic ones were badly damaged and were still being restored. We walked together down a long corridor, with her pointing out the different departments and showing me my office before turning into a small lobby leading into a newer section. This newer section seemed to have been recently attached to the building, as its style clashed with the architectural style of the other section. The old building was Gothic-style, with oil paintings from the seventeenth century on its walls, golden baroque-style ornaments, high walls intersecting the ceiling, windows embedded in stucco, and glass chandeliers that broke the sunlight into delightful little rainbows. As for the new section, it looked more like a hospital, with its bare walls, glass doors with metal framing, and electrical lighting that distributed light evenly.

We passed through a double glass door and stepped into a small room where we signed some papers. The employee scanned my fingerprints, pressed some buttons on his computer, then pointed at the door. I placed my finger on a small pad that beeped and opened the gate. We found ourselves in a glass-encased room. Maria smiled.

"Excuse us, Professor, you know the procedures to get into the restoration department: no dust or organic substances are allowed."

I smiled while remembering the status of the restoration department at Alexandria University where employees enjoyed their breakfast on the table next to the monuments that were being restored. One day, I smelled a real hideous odour emanating from the restoration department. I thought that the mummies had rotted, only to realize that one of the employees had brought in Fesikh (fermented, salted, and dried fish, a traditional Egyptian dish). As they ate it with great relish, the odour of the fermented fish quickly raised my concerns about the state of their work. The dean mocked me, insinuating that I was a foreigner from Cambridge University. Then he boastfully trivialized the incident, explaining to me that Fesikh is of Pharaonic heritage, and so the best place to eat it is in the restoration department.

Maria brought two plastic bags out of a small niche in the wall. She gave me one; it contained slippers made of strong plastic which you could wear over shoes, a thin medical mask, and rubber gloves. I laughed as I watched her turning into a nurse getting ready for the operating room. She laughed right along with me.

I was a little bit disappointed when, after entering the restoration section, I realized I would not be able to check the manuscripts directly. Professor Carlo, the person in charge of the restoration, gave me detailed photocopies of the readable texts of the manuscripts. He told me that a lot of the restoration efforts depended on the translation, as it allowed them to put the lines and the words in their correct context. Some pages were almost crumbled, and efforts were underway to treat the papyrus so that it could regain its firmness while being flexible.

We were overwhelmed for half an hour by technical and procedural details being thrown at us until finally I was given a high-quality photocopy of the mysterious Demotic manuscript. The first lines were clear and contained an immediate, unexpected surprise: this manuscript was different from any other Demotic manuscript I had ever seen.

It seemed like we really had a unique archeological discovery, and I believed we needed to call for an urgent meeting with all team members. This discovery was the equivalent of Darwin finding a creature proving the link between man and monkey.

. . . . .

After four hours in the prestigious meeting room, Professor Roberto Geovany and fourteen scientists and academics with different nationalities stood still. I took a deep breath then walked to the front of the room.

"Gentlemen, it seems like we really have made an unexpected discovery, not only because it belongs to the thirteenth century and it is written in a script we thought had disappeared in the sixth- or seventh-century AD, but also because it is written in a way we have never seen before. We know that Demotic is the third form of old Egyptian writing. It is an alphabetic writing and not a language used by people in their daily life in the period from eighth-century BC to fourth-century AD. I don't need to remind you, of course, that's where the Greek word *demo* comes from. We know that the ancient Egyptians in Roman times used the Greek alphabet for writing instead of the Demotic one. Later known as Coptic, it kept seven letters from the Demotic alphabet to imitate the Coptic sounds which do not have an equivalent in Greek..."

Doctor Hussein El Jaafary interrupted me, "Set your introductions aside, son; they are a waste of time. Everyone in the room knows the main principles you are talking about, even me, even though I am not specialized in studying old Egyptian history and writing."

Professor Geovany glared at him. While I did not like Doctor Hussein's provocative tone either, I continued as if I had not heard him.

"All the researchers classify the Coptic language as an independent one, separate from old Egyptian. Maybe they consider it an extension that borrowed some terms and distorted its pronunciation, or used some grammatical rules which were used in old Egyptian. But this document is the first known manuscript that was written in Coptic using Demotic script."

There were gasps of astonishment throughout the room. Professor Geovany groaned, saying, "That's why no one could decipher the manuscript symbols before. The words seem meaningless."

"Exactly, Professor. This manuscript was written the same way people using Facebook and text messages in our age write Arabic text using Latin characters. No one would be able to understand the written text unless he knew both languages."

"This means that you can translate this manuscript, Doctor Daniel, since you can read Demotic writing and understand Coptic as well," Professor Geovany said.

"To a certain extent, yes. But the exact translation is dependent on the restoration of the complete manuscript and knowing the overall context of this text. We have before us a unique manuscript; there is nothing like it in the archaeological research world. I believe that the efforts of Doctor Hussein El Jaafary to scrutinize the Arabic manuscripts will greatly help in the progress of translating the Demotic text," I answered enthusiastically.

Doctor Jaafary frowned and asked, "Do you believe that the Demotic/Coptic is a translation of the Arabic texts?"

"I do not think so… The Arabic text is longer. The Demotic text is written by someone other than Najm El Din Ibn Al Bitar, someone who wrote by the name of Youness the Egyptian. We will try to search for the relationship between the two and determine how these unique documents came to Italy. Did this take place at the same time when the manuscripts were written, or at a later time?"

Before the meeting came to an end, Doctor Hussein El Jaafari dropped a bomb of his own. He stood up and coughed to get everyone's attention.

"By the way, as for the green city mentioned in the manuscript of Ibn Al Bitar, where he said his mother found it during her travels from Egypt to Damascus..."

Professor Geovany interrupted him, "Yes, Doctor, we assumed that it was just imagination. We cannot recognize information provided by an unknown person as a historical fact. We do not know anything about a historical town in the time of Moses of this description."

"In fact, this town exists in a known text of a famous historian belonging to this age. Taqey El Din Al Maqrizi mentioned the description of this green town almost exactly in his book *Behavior to Know the State of the Kings*. I reviewed the original copy of this book and I found the description of this town as it is mentioned by Ibn Al Bitar in his manuscript," Doctor Jaafary said.

Usually academic meetings end with the hum of quiet conversation and the scraping of chairs, but this time rich enthusiasm filled the room as thoughts travelled to the remote sands of the desert where an ancient city was buried along with its secrets. The ancient papyrus in our hands was much like Aladdin's enchanted lamp; whenever we swiped the dust from it, the genie came out to revive dead words written in a language understood by barely anyone in the modern age.

"BUT PETER REPLIED, "MAY YOUR SILVER PERISH WITH YOU, BECAUSE YOU THOUGHT YOU COULD BUY THE GIFT OF GOD WITH MONEY! YOU HAVE NO PART OR SHARE IN OUR MINISTRY, BECAUSE YOUR HEART IS NOT RIGHT BEFORE GOD."

ACTS 8, VERSE 20/21

Immigrant to the Sky

You can start your trip but you will never know how it will end. I am Youness the Egyptian. I took off my secular gown at the gates of the Qalamoun monastery and lost my physical freedom in the fields of Cyprus. My body fluctuates between time and space but my soul will remain aloft eager to Heaven. Truth, justice, and love, if man weighed them in his hand, he would not find the weight of silver and gold, or even the power of the sword. Gold is heavier and iron is tougher than the hand created from clay and burdened by sin, but the spirit does not weigh the material with this mortal scale; the spirit knows the value of things by being closer to the kingdom of Heaven. Blessed are those who liberated the soul from the clay of the body and its sins.

The first paragraph of the Demotic manuscript did not take a long time to translate. Luckily, Youness the Egyptian was clearly the author of this document. But I spent a long time on the next mysterious lines that contained incomplete symbols. I hoped the restoration process could clear this up so that I would be able to put these symbols in their context. A clearly written word stopped me, as its meaning was not clear at all. It could be pronounced *charatonah* or something like that... Perhaps the writer of the manuscript meant *achartonah*, a word of Greek origin meaning *the position of the hand* but used in the Coptic language to denote giving the seal of the holy spirit to someone, or, more precisely, drawing priests in their religious positions.

Youness the Egyptian wrote:

> **Simon the magician and his followers are chasing me everywhere. The word Lord was bought and sold, monasteries of salvation uttered the faithful people... There is no place for the ascetics in the fryers; the wool robes were replaced with gowns made of silk.**

Although I was good at Coptic, Coptic history was not my field of expertise. I asked Maria to research the conditions of the Copts in thirteenth-century Egypt and to look for the name Youness the Egyptian in the lists of Egyptian monks in monasteries.

The research was exhausting. This name was common among the monks of the thirteenth century, specifically because of the good reputation of Pope Youness the Sixth. He managed the Patriarchate of Alexandria for about thirty years before he died in 1216. He was ascetic and charitable, people of the Church loved him, and he was respected by Muslims and the Sultan. The papal seat remained empty after him for almost twenty years until a pastor named Dawood Bin Laqlaq ascended to the papacy in a mysterious way in 1235 during the reign of King Alkamel Al Ayoubi. The pope sold church positions with money in so-called *Simony*, named after Simon the Magician who, as mentioned in the Book of Acts of the Apostles, wanted to bribe Peter the Apostle to give him the Holy Spirit. Peter rejected this offer and told him, "Let your silver perish with thee because you thought to acquire the gift of God with dirhams. Thou hast neither part nor lot in this matter because your heart is not upright before God."

It was clear that Youness the Egyptian was a monk that rebelled against the selling of religious positions. Rainwater erased several paragraphs of his manuscript, but the last paragraph in the first papyrus roll was the scream of a soul tormented through eternity:

> *He who has ears, let him hear! At the gates of the cities I knocked, residents did not respond. I searched in the markets and found nothing but fraud and deception. When the kingdom is sold with silver and necks are subject to the sword, comes the beast mentioned at the time of Revelation. People buy and sell, parading in the markets and drowning in sins, not realizing that tomorrow, they are going to kneel before the dragon. Fear God and give Him glory, because His judgment hour has come, and worship the Maker of Heaven and Earth, the sea and springs of water8.*

---

[8] This last phrase is from Revelations 7:14.

The Third Voyage

Damietta, 1269

Praise be to God, the first before origin and rebirth, the last after everything perishes. He knows all. He never forgets who remembered Him, he who thanks Him will not be harmed, he who begs Him will never be disappointed.

We are destined to travel. We travel along the years, children turning into young men and men turning into elderly ones... In our travels through countries and regions between deserts and seas, we miss our beloved ones and our homeland.

Ten years have passed since our escape from the swords of the Tatars. We travelled among cities and migrants. My mother died and did not reach safety in Egypt; Sheikh Yusuf buried her on the road between Homs and Deraa. I mourned her while travelling, as we did not even have time to cry at her grave.

Faces and cities changed around us for ten years. God raised kings and humiliated others. People died; others were born. His will happened in the world, no one replaced nor changed it. The Tatars were defeated in the Levant by the Sultan Qutuz, who did not even have time to celebrate as his Mamluks killed him and took over the throne. Muslim countries remained with no caliphate until the Sultan of Egypt Al-Zaher Baibars chose an

Abbasid prince and made him a caliphate and sent him to rule the Islamic world from the ruins of Baghdad destroyed by Hulaku and Tatar armies. But the caliphate was killed there. It is said that the Tatars killed him or that the assassins incited him, and so the sultan assigned another Abbasid prince (distant grandson of the Prophet Mohamed) to be the new caliphate in Cairo. The sultan was the one who created and owned the caliphate. Those who have the sword and the caliphate have the throne and power, which is what happened to the sultan of the Mamluks in Egypt to become the ruler of all the countries of the East.

The sword owns the neck only, but not what is above or below. The caliphate gown can cover the minds and wrap the hearts. The Tatars owned the sharp sword and they owned half of the Islamic lands. But the absence of the Lord's gown sent all of what they owned into the wind. Today, after the caliphate state returned under the sword of Sultan Al Zahir Baibars, the people who talked about the end of the world are no longer. Stories about the perishing are gone, and talks of the Resurrection Day have returned. People know it and do not expect it; they believe in it but do not wait for it. They think it is going to happen in another time with another people. People with the successor of God's messenger among them do not deserve to be convulsed by the horrors of the Resurrection and Judgment Day.

At Damietta harbour, when it was time to leave, I thought about my mother telling me to go after my father in the Franks' land. She made me swear on her deathbed that the first thing I would do when I became a young man is to look for my royal blood across the huge sea. I have land, family, and heritage there. Money is not important; a look into my eyes is sufficient. I inherited his blue eyes and facial features, and I have his golden ring which carries the mysterious noble badge.

"I did not get pregnant by adultery, son. I did not disgrace you or myself. Meet your father and ask him. Look into his eyes to find yours. Your uncle is still the Frank King, and he witnessed our marriage."

My mother was fighting death whilst holding my hand and asking me to swear in front of her. I swore without realizing what I was committing myself to.

I spent a week in the port of Damietta waiting for the ship to move towards the Franks' land. I wandered each day through the city without leaving it. The Chinese silk, the coffee from Yemen, the Indian spices, the Persian carpets; yellow, dark, black, and red faces; eyes talking in different ways; different terms and accents, but speaking the same language of money. Gold is what brings East and West together, what unites the hearts of merchants, and what brings the Sultan's soldiers and ship captains coming from afar to seek wealth in the markets of Damietta.

All the gold I had was my inherited golden ring with its mysterious symbol. I hid it in my underwear as I was afraid of thieves. Sheikh Yusuf told me last year when he knew that I intended to leave, "Gold is the traveller's fund and his death, too."

He said this to me then took the ring from my hand and put it in the wood coals that we were warming ourselves with. When the ring glowed, he put a piece of wood between my teeth and told me to bite it. He then marked the ring's symbol on my left arm, and then sprinkled some cold dust on the painful and still smoking mark. I fainted from the pain. When I woke up, I found my left arm tied with a bandage of honey and willow paper. This mark is to be evidence of my identity if the ring gets lost or stolen. The mysterious mythological creature blowing fire burns on my arm forever; the mark of my father is on my arm like his blood is in my veins, despite the physical distance between us.

In Damietta, travelling is not for everyone. Preachers speak at Friday prayers about the land of the infidels and the land of faith. Damietta lies on the boundary between two worlds, the last land of Islam, separated by the vast sea from the land of the infidels. The infidels' ships come and go but leave the Islamic lands with nothing but goods collected from everywhere. They carry baggage, not humans, as Muslim traders are not allowed to journey beyond Damietta. The profit should be split evenly between everyone and the Sultan, who owns the intersection of the two lands. He had an agreement with Genoa merchants in the Franks' country that they were to be the only ones authorized to transport goods from Damietta to their country.

People all around Egypt believed that the Franks were all the same. But people who come into contact with a lot of Frank ships know that they are made up of different races and nationalities. Amongst themselves they have divisive wars, rival kingdoms, and cities fighting over the spoils of war and trade.

I carried my goods which would allow me to get on the ship: medical herbs and mixtures that combine to form secret perfumes. I convinced the Genoese captain that my merchandise was not just baggage that he could carry and pay a price for, but that I should be there too in order to be beneficial and profitable. Without the veterinarian,[9] the herbs would be useless. The captain will have one third of the profit when he takes me back to Damietta next summer and the collector of the sultan in Damietta will get another third. We stamped a contract with this agreement, which I left at the port office. This contract will be my only lifeboat in the land of the infidels, as it gives the captain the responsibility to bring me back safely to my home to pay the Sultan's share.

The ship has two big sails and a high bow and a disgusting smell. There is mould everywhere, and the smell only worsens as I go deeper into the belly of the boat. I descended with one of the sailors to the huge store deep inside the ship to leave the goods there, next to a big load of spices and different items shipped from one side of the world to the other. Almost suffocating, I went up to the ship deck. The sailor who accompanied me was tall, blond,

---

[9]   The word Bitar in Arabic means veterinary.

and had three fingers missing from his right hand. His beard and clothes smelled like vomit. I asked him to guide me to the sleeping quarters; he laughed, took me to large hall near the deck, and told me that passengers and sailors gather here if it became stormy or started to rain. During a calm night, the deck is better and quieter, but I have to tie myself with rope while sleeping so as not to be thrown into the sea by a sudden wave.

I was the only Arab passenger on the ship. All the other passengers and sailors were Franks. They differed in height, appearance, clothing, and even language; but they all smelled the same, a mixture of vomit and mould, probably the smell of the infidels I was told about by one of the eunuchs working with the tax collector. He was laughing and saying that Islam has blessed the Muslims through washing five times every day, as well as after menstruating and sexual intercourse; but Franks are infidels that do not even wash from impurity, carousing in drinking alcohol, and eating pork, which makes them smell this way.

Perhaps there is some truth behind what he said, though I lived with Coptic people from Egypt and they were of a good smell. The Coptic wash at least once every week and attend Sunday memorial prayer dressed up and as thoroughly clean as Muslims at Friday prayers. In our country, types of perfumes are endless and used by rich and poor alike. In public restrooms, special recipes are used to massage the body to eliminate sweat and get rid of dead skin.

In the next days, when I found out that the Franks had no public restrooms, I was astonished. I trembled to go to this desolate, dirty world.

When the departure time came, I was not the only Arabic passenger. At the last moment, another passenger boarded the ship. He did not have goods nor the features of the merchants. His luggage was a big sack containing supplies for the trip: dates, bread, and dried figs. He was thin, strong-bodied, of average height, and dark-skinned. He had the looks of a Persian Kurd. Under his black turban, two deep eyes stared back, filled with secrets. I welcomed him but he treated me coldly. All I knew was his name: Hassan El Musly; that's how the captain introduced him to me. It seemed like the captain knew him pretty well. I did not know that I was to have a shared destiny with him in the coming days.

After an hour of sailing, the captain gathered us and explained that the trip would take two weeks. From now on, he had the right to own the life of every man on board. He could order the death penalty for anyone without even showing reason. He would not accept anything except complete obedience and we had to swear in front of him while touching the sharp edge of his sword: "God is in the Sky; Captain is on the ship until we arrive safely."

We sailed with the sun shining behind us. I was struck by seasickness. Nothing stayed in my stomach. The smell of vomit was chasing me, the infidels' land giving me its smell even before I touched its soil. After two days of suffering I became a little bit better; I was able to stand and eat. The sailors mocked the Muslims for not being able to sail the seas, as Hassan and myself were the terribly sick ones. But I became better, whereas he was getting worse. He had fever, chills, and diarrhea. On the fourth day, the captain checked his chest and found pink blotches; he was shocked, and gave orders to exile Hassan at the end of the ship. He warned everyone not to come close to him or deal with him, announcing that if these pink blotches turned into dark red ones he would throw Hassan in the sea so as not to infect everyone.

I pitied Hassan for the destiny awaiting him; I asked the captain to allow me to medicate him. He warned me that if I got infected too, I would face the same fate. I went down to the store and brought up from my goods some rhubarb, pomegranate peel, powder of paper willow, and antimony. I mixed them together, put some of it in a piece of cloth, and put it on Hassan's head, on his chest, and in his mouth. I made cuts in his head; a lot of poisoned blood came out. I kept changing the pieces of cloth and massaging his body with lemon and senna, until the fever was gone. After two days he started to look better.

"Are you a veterinarian or a doctor?" the captain asked me, laughing.

"What heals horses works with human beings, and what works with people in the sultans' lands works in the land of the Franks."

But the captain did not hear my reply. His eyes had caught three ships appearing between the fog, driven fast by the wind toward our ship. The captain shouted, ordering his men to pull the spinnaker and turn the rudder against the direction of the wind to move as quickly as possible. I did not understand the panic that ensured among the sailors. Hassan weakly explained, "They are the allies of the Venetians."

Once more I did not understand, so he elaborated while pulling a sharp dagger from his clothes, "They are pirates. If you do not have a sword, then go fetch one. Before this sun sets, all our heads might be hanging on that far mast."

Trip of Eagerness

Rome, 11 February 2011.

Tears of joy.
I used to hear this expression a lot. I watched people in movies crying out of joy, but I was never convinced. I never understood that feeling which fills the eyes with tears while the heart is dancing from happiness.

On that day, for the first time in my life, I experienced this feeling.

Around 4:00 p.m. I was indulging in Ibn Al Bitar when Maria burst into my office: "Mubarak stepped down!"

I raised my eyes towards her, stunned. The last thing I saw yesterday on the news was a stubborn and stupid President Mubarak talking with the same cold face, as always imposing the same ideas and terms under which he has ruled Egypt for decades. I was thankful for Ibn Al Bitar for distracting me from the news and the incidents taking place in Tahrir Square, where protestors raised their shoes in anger and declared that they were going to break into the presidential palace. I found out that the previous night thousands of protestors marched from Tahrir Square towards the residence of the president while in Alexandria, protesters marched towards the presidential palace in the city. I was depressed by the analysis of the newscasters on TV, who cheered at Mubarak's speech as always, stating that it was an absolute victory for the revolution — using this term probably for the first time. Their analysis warned of the bloodbath that could fill Egypt if the so-called troublemakers insisted on inflaming the situation. I woke up this morning, boycotting the TV thanks to Ibn Al Bitar; submerging myself instead in my work until Maria made her entrance into my office with this stunning news.

"Vice-President Omar Soliman announced a few seconds ago that Mubarak stepped down. Congratulations, Professor; the revolution succeeded and you eliminated the tyrant!"

Surely, I flinched. At least, I felt like I did when she hugged me to congratulate me. My body was trembling, my voice was blocked with tears, my chest was tight... After a while the team members came, and the warmth of their congratulations melted the ice in my eyes. I cried and cried, tears of joy pouring down my face. Bottles of champagne were opened. Professor Geovany invited all of us to celebrate, and he did not forget to point out one of the bottles that contained alcohol-free champagne for me.

Sunset offered a fun atmosphere in the streets of Rome, which were usually decorated for the nighttime. But this night was very special. The night covered Rome with a festive mood like those that take place when its national football team wins the European Cup. Lots of fans pass, singing the songs of victory and waving flags. Smiling faces share the same joy. This time it was not the Romanian team that won, and it was not the orange flags that were covering the celebrants. Instead, black, white, and red lines adorned the flags on this night. I did not think that many Egyptians were living in Rome, but after a while, I found different Arabic dialects amongst the celebrants: Tunisian, Iraqi, Lebanese, Palestinian, as well as Italians and tourists sharing this moment of happiness.

The screens in the coffee shops continued displaying the details of the victory, as if repeating the match. Tahrir Square scored an international goal, and Egypt was crowned with a special victory on this night. For the first time I saw Omar Soliman, Head of Intelligence, reading the speech announcing Mubarak's decision with a face filled with sorrow. The Italian subtitles did not prevent me from translating the speech to Maria who was wondering who that grim man standing behind Omar Soliman was: was he a known official in Egypt? Did his presence inside the cadre in this intrusive manner imply something? I could not reply, but translated to her what came in the next scenes of the Egyptians celebrating in Tahrir Square. She asked me about the singing that could be heard both in Tahrir Square and in Rome.

"It means: Raise your head up high; you are Egyptian!"

I tried to translate the meaning of what the protesters were shouting on television.

"Indeed! Egyptians have the right to be proud today. The civilized way with which they rebelled will change a lot in the world in the coming years. This is probably the new September 11th, but this time in a positive way!" she replied cheerfully.

I looked into Maria's face, which was even more beautiful because of the joy she was emanating. I had gotten used to her Japanese features which no longer clashed with the vivid way she expressed her feelings. She is like Mediterranean people, who use voice, facial gestures, and hand movements, in contrast with the mysterious conservative way that Asian people act, with the same polite smile potentially expressing either happiness, anger, love, or pessimism.

I was surprised by her overwhelming enthusiasm and sincere happiness. Why was she so enthusiastic about what was happening in Egypt? I understood why Professor Geovany was enthusiastic: he lived in Egypt for many long years and had a close friendship with my father. He was aware of what my father suffered because he too opposed the regime. But Maria had never been to Egypt and did not have conflict with Mubarak or his regime.

"Why are you celebrating with all this happiness?" I asked her.

Her wide smile turned into a mysterious Japanese one, and she said, "I have reasons why it makes me happy when any dictator falls, and why I feel happy for anyone who won an honourable war for his freedom. It is you who should answer this question. Since you have landed in Italy, you have been very shy talking about what is happening in Egypt. You only comment neutrally, even to the most enthusiastic questions. It is you, Professor, who needs to answer why are you were suddenly so happy when you heard the news of Mubarak's fall."

I did not reply.

Two hours later, alone in darkness of my hotel room, I found the answer in the mirror. This time it was not tears of joy I found in my eyes, but rather tears of longing for the one I got these eyes from. My father was gone and yet his eyes accompanied me, looking at me every time I looked in a mirror. His friends said that I did not inherit anything from his features except his pure blue eyes. Maybe I was only really noticing on this day, or maybe I had always noticed. This might be why I chose to treat my nearsightedness with dark-coloured contact lenses that hid the inherited blue eyes, but never hid the true look.

My father died five years ago. But he had lived through similar events in Tahrir Square in his lifetime, some forty years ago, chanting for freedom and paying for it without regret, despite the blamers (which included my mother).

I took off my dark-coloured contact lenses, slipping my glasses on instead. I started searching the internet for a collection of poems from Amal Dunqul. I was looking for the "Stone Cake" poem in particular. I had heard it from my father thousands of times but I had never felt it until today:

> *The exhausted clock ticking*
> *His kind mother raised*
> *Her eyes ...*
> *The rifle butts pushed him inside the vehicle.*

I do not know how many times rifle butts pushed my father into police cars. These dawn visitors were frequent guests in our lives. They came in their own chosen moment, when the night fell, when my family's warmth filled the room, and the caring touch of my father gave me a sense of security. Behind closed doors and in between waking and sleeping, spouses whispered in worry. Then the storm would strike the house. I would be in tears, freaking out, looking for my mother to hold me. Chilled bare feet, heart trembling in silence for fear of making even a faint sigh that would disturb the scene.

Hands slapped him...
Hand of God got him inside the experiment
Poked by the eyes of the investigator...
Until his skin erupted blood and answers!

In January 1972, my father was a young professor at the Faculty of Archaeology when thousands of students from Cairo University held huge demonstrations. History did not mention these demonstrations as they deserved to be mentioned. It was dropped on purpose from books and from records. If it weren't for the famous poem of Amal Dunqul, no one would have known the truth of what happened.

My father would say, "Neither Amal Dunqul nor the other intellectuals joined us in the fight. The majority of the participants were college students who were provoked by the declarations of President Anwar Al Sadat about the Fog Year. He had promised that immediately after becoming president, 1971 would be the decisive year in the confrontation with Israel and the restoration of Sinai... Protestors were just unarmed students, their only guns were enthusiasm and hope. They did not throw stones but jingles at the soldiers. Writers and intellectuals were sitting at Ezavitch Café overlooking Tahrir Square. Their sympathy with the protesting students was no more than nodding their heads and smiling. Then they went home early before the fighting started."

Time sounded harsh
The radio in the café broadcasts his speeches
The worn-out speeches
About the advocates of riots
They are turning around
Getting on fire around the Stone Cake
Around the monument
Candlestick of anger
Glowing in the night...
Their voices are sweeping the remaining darkness
Singing for the birth night of a new Egypt!

I heard the story from my father dozens of times. It took place on the third week of January 1972. The students had filled the corridors of the university with demonstrations denouncing the position of President Sadat about war and the decisive year that had passed without any resolution. On January 24th, a campaign of arrests took place targeting student leaders; the rest of the students went to the university to find it closed. The government decided to start the mid-year vacation early to prevent these demonstrations. But dozens, then hundreds, and finally thousands of students crowded in front of the university gates, much like dew drops turning into a flood. Enthusiastic and angry, the students decided to walk to Tahrir Square, the biggest square in Cairo, and stage a sit-in below the large stone monument which was named *Stone Cake* by Amal Dunqul in his poem.

My father had said: "This monument was located in a circular garden at the centre of Tahrir Square. It is said that it goes back to the age of the late King Farouk, who wanted to put in the middle of the square a solemn statue of his grandfather the Khedive Ismael. Thus, the monument was constructed; but the military coup vanquished King Farouk in 1952, and the idea of the statue was scrapped. It is said that there would be a statue placed upon the stone monument that would glorify the struggle of the Egyptian people. Throughout the age of President Nasser, there was widespread news about the statues that could be placed above the monument: a statue embodying the martyrs of the Suez Canal; the High Dam; freedom... They changed the name of the square in an instant, but they have spent years trying to create something to cover the abandoned stone monument. When Nasser died, Sadat announced that the statue would be of one of the timeless leaders, Gamal Abdel Nasser. But all these projects were just words in the newspapers. The monument remained as it were until the students' 1972 sit-in."

My dad always laughed when he remembered the story of the stone monument, saying, "Interestingly, the memorial stone was later completely removed from the square, pulled out from its roots at the beginning of the era of Mubarak. It was said at that time that this was in order to complete underground drilling. But the fact is that they were afraid of the stone monument immortalized in Amal Dunqul's poem."

The student protestors stayed in the square after sunset. My father followed them and was most likely the only member of the faculty who joined them. The cold January night did not freeze the enthusiasm in their chests; they were warmed by songs and chants and hand-holding. Hours crawled slowly by with the night coming, which brought in steady throngs of soldiers who surrounded the field.

It is five o'clock
The soldiers appeared as a circle of shields and helmets of war
Here they are now approaching slowly...
Slowly they come from every direction
And singers - in the Stone Cake - constrict
And diverge
Like a heartbeat!
Yelling out loud
Warming from the cold and frigid darkness
Singing out loud facing the approaching guards

Grasping their tender and miserable hands
To become a fence that repels bullets!
Bullets ...
Bullets ...
And Oh ...
Singing: "We sacrifice ourselves for you, O Egypt,
we sacrifice ourselves for y..."
The throat falls silent
The silence falls with your name - O Egypt - to the ground
Only the dead body and the screaming remains
On the dark place

By dawn, the square was completely empty. The twenty thousand students who participated in the protest were swept away by the soldiers' batons and bullets. YouTube, Twitter, or Facebook were not around to record what had happened. There was nothing mentioned in the newspapers other than the number of injured, killed, and arrested. Even the memory of my father would not satisfy anyone searching for details of the story. A soldier's baton knocked him out at the beginning of the intrusion, and so he didn't see the beating, killing, and dragging. The warmth in the square was replaced by the chill of prison and cruel investigations. Investigators were trying to discipline these kids, not to convict them or send them to trial. Weeks later, most of those arrested were released after being freed from the illusion of freedom by whips.

But my father was not one of these kids. He was a university professor and he was labelled forever with a record of being 'dangerous.' He was fired from the university; he did return after the October War, but was kept away from the students, finding instead a new path in excavations and archaeological research projects.

"Life is nothing but a bunch of incompatible details, puzzle pieces to be put in their correct place to revive shreds of pottery, pieces of stones, ancient inscriptions; telling stories that got lost among the years," my father always said.

That's how my father ended his days, removing dust from his clothes and narrating the details of the dig he was working on. We shared winter nights behind windows covered with raindrops. In my childhood I loved the winter seasonal storms, as much as I hated the storms of the soldiers. The winter seasonal storms used to clean the streets of people staying up late and warm the house with the stories of my father. The soldiers' storm blew at dawn to throw the cover away from those sleeping and took away a sense of security. My mother swallowed her tears in panic. She begged the officer to leave the door closed, as behind it lay a child suffering from a fever. Thunder hit and lightning glowed and a strict military order echoed in the walls of the house. Soldiers moved in organized chaos. The humiliation was not complete until mother and her two children were standing barefoot in pyjamas. People behind the closed windows were listening to whispers while checking their safety latches. The wide eyes ignored the line of prisoners brought through the darkness of the night. My mother's eyes hugged her sick son under the rain. Mother and sons were transported by the roar of an old car like an old mixer, and jabbed by tough hands. Cold bit at their bones. They waited for hours on the floor. An old sergeant pitied them and brought them an old tattered blanket that smelled of urine and vomit.

In the pale morning, the sun was ashamed to shine but still sent faint white rays to the eastern horizon. The kind taxi driver agreed to pick up the three who were barefoot in front of the police station and take them to the hospital without getting paid. He was probably wondering what had happened. At the end of his day, he probably felt pity while narrating the incident to his wife. But during the ride, he fought his curiosity as if afraid to ask for an answer that he knew would haunt him forever.

Two days later, my eight-year-old twin died. My mother never forgave my father for this. The ground itself wept when it welcomed the small body. The loss of her son dug a dark hole inside my mother's heart, while my father secluded himself forever in the darkness of grief.

They say time heals all wounds, but my mother's wound was too deep. It did not heal until she died after years of separation from my father.

"Did you not have enough? What did your delusions do to you? The utopia you are clinging to is only inhabited with idiots." This sentence almost slipped from my mouth to my father, but I never dared to say it.

At a young age, I graduated with distinction and became a lecturer at the Faculty of Archeology. I was waiting for security approvals to travel to London to get a scholarship at Cambridge University, but my dreams of education collided with my father's security file.

The restrictions I had at my university did not end: my scholarship rested with the dean and the security approvals that would not come. I did not say a word of blame to my father. But he saw the silent blame in my eyes.

He was recalling some of memories of Tahrir Square with his old friends. After they left, he answered the question I did not ask:

"Son, you know I spent years searching for Alexander the Great's grave. I did not find it; maybe I will never find it. But do you think these years were spent in vain?"

He paused for a moment, then continued without waiting for my reply: "O my son, age does not have a price. The age is more precious than money or ignorance. But freedom and conscience are more precious than everything. They are priceless.

"We are digging old graves. We wipe tons of sand with toothbrushes just to remove dust from a word that was once spoken, but nobody heard it.

"When you give freedom to a word that has been forgotten for thousands of years, you can prove that nothing is wasted.

"Nothing is wasted even if it was buried for years or hidden by the mountains or eaten by the oppressors. Nothing in this world is equal to a right word uttered by a free conscience when the moment of choice comes."

I never forgot this conversation with my father. On this day I lived it all over again, as his words turned into a ship carrying me on a voyage from longing to the distant world that Tahrir Square had revived.

Protestors who went to Tahrir Square eighteen days ago did not take with them toothbrushes to remove dust from the footprints of their ancestors. They did not know that the footprints were once watered with blood. They did not find the Stone Cake to cling to. The majority certainly did not know that they were reviving a forgotten ritual that was forcibly removed from the history books. And yet they chose Tahrir Square and the 25th of January to be their symbol of victory.

Time and place always repeat. They do this until the end. They surfed the square facing soldiers with chants. They paid sacrifices, hugged their dead colleagues, and came closer to God through blood, until God finally accepted their prayers and good deeds.

My father was right. Age is priceless as long as the free conscience looks like the phoenix. Both may be burnt to ashes, then resurrected once again.

· · · · ·

Next morning, the ringing of the phone woke me. It was Maria whose tone, as usual, was laced with great zeal.

"The gazelle leather bag that was found with the cache, well... the results of the radiocarbon and laboratory analysis came out. Prepare yourself for a huge surprise, Professor. No, no, I will not tell you over the phone. I will be waiting for you in the lobby."

About half an hour later, I passed in front of the information desk and found her, head buried in papers. Once she saw me, her face suddenly shone with even more excitement:

"O, che un nuovo look!"

I did not understand what she meant. What was this new look that was grabbing her attention?

"Your blue eyes, Professor! Your look is purer and more beautiful. Are these new lenses?"

I took out my glasses and slipped them on.

"On the contrary; I took out my contact lenses."

"How many secrets do you have, Professor?"

"Forget my secrets! We have the secrets of the cache to fill our days. What is surprising in the report of the radiocarbon?"

"Cappuccino e cornetto first. I did not have my breakfast yet and neither have you. In Rome, the day does not start before the morning coffee."

The vividness in her tone touched my heart, spreading a joy in the morning breath. I pretended to frown while accepting her order but it was clear I was kidding.

At the café, the smell of the cappuccino mixed with fresh baked goods wafted over us, but this did not make me forget the huge surprise that was presented to me by Maria Satriano. The report from the chemical laboratory was clear: the black greasy substance that was found in the cache consisted of organic substances that included human parts, while the radiocarbon report dated it back to 1300 BC. I frowned while trying to put the seemingly incompatible pieces of the puzzle together.

"We are talking about the remnants of the mummy of an unknown pharaoh who came to Italy in the thirteenth century, who crossed the sea and time and was accompanied by a person or persons of an unknown age. Maybe they were practicing black magic? I know that the use of ground pharaonic mummies was widespread in medicine in the Middle Ages. They used to believe mummies had magical power that could cure all disease…"

Maria interrupted me with a graceful movement and a funny smile while getting out another paper as if she were a delightful magician drawing marvels out of her sack.

"Hold onto your logic. You will need it to read the next report," she said.

I checked the paper which included a chemical analysis for another separate item from the leather bag.

"Weed! That's just what we need, weed!" I could not prevent myself from laughing out loud.

"It seems that we might need to have an expert from Interpol joining the team and not someone from UNESCO. This is probably the oldest drug trafficking gang in history. What is the opinion of Professor Geovany regarding these reports?" I continued.

"Professor Geovany is waiting for the restoration and translation of the rest of the manuscripts before he forms an opinion," Maria replied.

She was silent for a while then looked directly into my eyes while saying in soft voice, "The pleasure of archaeological research lies in its surprises, Professor Danny. I am thankful for the pleasure of working with you."

I was filled with a fresh feeling of happiness. Like a bird in the spring breeze, my heart danced with joy. This analogy seemed accurate to the greatest possible extent: just as the bird knows that spring is definitely coming and waits for its breeze, my heart was aware that inevitably its fate would be in the hands of Maria.

. . . . .

We arrived late at the academy, our eyes shining with that thrill unique to blossoming love.

"GLORY TO SATAN,
WHO IS WORSHIPPED BY THE WIND
WHO SAID NO FOR THOSE WHO SAID YES
WHO TAUGHT MAN TO TEAR THE NOTHINGNESS
HE WHO SAID NO, DID NOT DIE
HE REMAINED A SOUL IN ETERNAL PAIN."

EGYPTIAN POET AMAL DUNQUL (1969)

Transit in London

London, 2001 to 2004

When I specialized in studying Demotic manuscripts, I did not know that I would live my life travelling between capitals and continents. All around the world there were thousands of Demotic manuscripts and texts that had been smuggled from Egypt in different eras. Shreds of pottery, sheets of papyrus, pieces of bone or stone or patches of leather… Demotic was the means by which the common people wrote about their day-to-day lives, as its symbols and terminology were more versatile —exactly like the difference between vernacular and classical Arabic. While the hieroglyphics and hieratic were used in formal documents and on the walls of the temples, Demotic was used by the common people who had varying levels of knowledge and different abilities to write correctly. That's why the clues of every text differed depending on the person who wrote it, the dialect he used, his level of education, and his intellect. When I rode around in my father's car, that old orange Volkswagen, I found myself amused by what the lorry and taxi drivers wrote on their cars: "Oh bad people, stop envying me." "I was envied, but God saved me." There was a lot of slang, usually misspelled, and very local terms that no one can understand except those who lived in the same time and social context with the one who wrote it.

Demotic text looked like that to a great extent, although it was actually merged with the soil and sweat of ordinary hard-working people. Part of the joy in the translation of Demotic texts was that they were filled with misspelled words and violated grammatical rules to such an extent that translation depended on guesswork, trying to be close to the writer and understanding his social and intellectual reality. That is why there are hundreds of thousands of demotic texts in all the museums and universities of the world, but very few of them have been translated, and fewer experts who are capable of translating them. So, I used to travel a lot to help research centres, universities, and museums that owned treasure troves of old documents and shards of pottery which no one had ever translated.

During the last ten years, I have travelled among dozens of countries and cities. I have crossed seas and oceans carrying my country in my small backpack. Among all this travelling, London held my personal record of the longest consecutive period I stayed in one city. It exceeded even my beloved Alexandria where I did not stay for more than six consecutive months in the past ten years. It was only London that took three years of my life. I stayed with my ex-wife, Sarah, the British girl I met at the wrong time in my life. Sometimes I had difficulty remembering what she looked like. Memory has its own strange way to keep or drop memories.

I travelled to London ten years ago to run away from my father's eyes and get a PhD. Did my father know what I did? He never mentioned it. But I knew deep inside that he knew, and I wished he would forgive me.

My father was everything to me after my mother died. I agreed to share his world, which brought me two competitive things: Alexander the Great, and 'political activities' which implanted in my childhood and youth memories of pain and obstacles.

He used to wake up before sunrise to prepare my school breakfast. He refused to let old Nanny Attiyat do this. She had been my father's nanny only to reappear again in our lives after the death of my mother. My father would take me to the school bus before going to the excavation sites of Alexander the Great's tomb, a tomb for which he dedicated his life searching. I was the only student the bus did not drive directly home. Rather it drove me to different archaeological places in Alexandria: Kom El Shoqaffa, the Roman Theatre, tombs of El Anfoushi, Montazah Palace, Al Raa's Al Sawdaa...

But my favourite place was the Roman Theatre next to the railway station where my father or one of his assistants would wait for me. We would have lunch together and, when the sun was about to set, he would take me in his small orange Volkswagen to our home in the Al Azarita district... I used to believe, when I was a child, that my father made this car especially for the two of us, since it had only two doors and two seats. The front looked like a jovial face and its rounded roof looked like the ball that I loved to play with.

Archeological sites were my childhood playgrounds. Would any child miss a chance to play with dust in front of his father without getting in trouble? Playing with dust was my father's passion. His only condition was that I should wear a mask to protect my lungs. He taught me to be cautious and not touch my eyes with my soiled hands. He used to sit and, with extreme patience, displace piles of dirt with a toothbrush, sifting with his assistants and students tons of sand through a sieve that looked like the ones used by housewives for flour. He used to jump like a kid when he would find a piece of pottery, a chunk of marble, or an old coin at the bottom of the sieve; regardless of how many items he had already found that day.

The first archeological piece I found was in the excavations of the Romanian theatre. It is exhibited now in the Greek-Romanian museum in Alexandria: a tiny Tanagra statue, its length not exceeding the length of a child's palm. I found it while playing in a pile of rubble brought in from an old bathroom, which had been waiting for its turn to be sieved. The statue looked like a doll of a beautiful woman with clear features; I only had to blow the dust away to see her colourful clothes. The childish joy that flooded me harmonized with the feelings of my father as he took off the dignity of the great professor and joined his young child in playing with a two-thousand-year-old toy.

The mysterious symbols of Demotic, Coptic, and Greek alphabets were my childhood companions. I drew them before knowing how they are pronounced. My father was used to writing small cards for me with the names of various things; everything in our house had a tag with its name using Demotic and Greek alphabets as well as Arabic. When I became a bit older, he started sending me short messages in the same way:

"Excuse me, beloved Daniel, I will have to leave for few weeks. Do not worry. Be obedient and Nanny Attiyat will take care of everything."

Sometimes I would wake up in the morning to find this type of message. I would decode its symbols, then rebel and refuse to eat the breakfast that was made by Nanny Attiyat until she would remind me of my father's instructions. This would make me, however unwillingly, eat my breakfast. Sometimes my father's absence would extend for quite a while. At times, Nanny Attiyat would come with me to live with my father's friend, Professor Roberto Geovany and his wife Signorina Kiara, who lived nearby in the Al Azarita neighbourhood. They always welcomed me with toys and sweets. I used to call them *Zio* Roberto and *Zia* Kiara, which meant *Uncle* Roberto and *Aunt* Kiara in Italian, as they helped to fill the void of the family members that were missing from my barren family tree.

My father's sudden absences were irregular. Sometimes he would return home at the end of the day, other times he would disappear for weeks. Once, he was away for three whole months. He returned with a long dusty beard, shaggy hair, and sticky eyes. He shaved, took a shower, and then became cheerful once more, taking me in his orange car for a special outing.

Gradually I realized the secret behind my father's absences. I understood why he put me in my bed and always refused to sleep beside me whenever I insisted. I knew why he left all the rooms and slept on a comfortable sofa next to the front door of the apartment, with a small bag beside it, prepared by Nanny Attiyat. Childhood curiosity made me look through the bag to find some underwear, a towel, a toothbrush, toothpaste, soap, canned tuna and salmon, and a package of dates and dried fruits. My father's life was full of departures and the supplies for these trips were in this bag which was always ready for the mysterious dawn visitors. Every night, my father slept on his sofa waiting for them, opening the door before harsh hands would knock and awaken the household.

I do not know exactly when I realized the complete truth. Part of me knew all along with the gloomy memories of my brother's death... the imprisoned breaths of Nanny Attiyat while she was preparing my school breakfast or her reactions when I would ask her when my father was coming back. Ironically, some of my schoolmates knew the truth before me. There was innuendo, singing, whispering, hints, laughter, and sidetalk that stopped suddenly when I would pay attention. When I grew older, innuendo took a more violent and aggressive form. Every time the television would display the movie *El Karnak*, the name 'Farag' became a means to torture and humiliate me by the bullies in my class. Farag was the full-bodied detective who raped the heroine of the film, Soaad Hosny, inside the prison in one of the most famous scenes in political cinema.

"Do you know what happens to the detainees in the state security office?" one student asked another.

The answer, along with a blatant laugh, whipped me:

"Hahahaha, Farag awaits them there! Oh Farag!"

It was only when someone passed by me and yelled "Farag!" that the bullies would mock me and laugh at me. Then I would start an unfair fight that would send me home with ripped clothes and a broken heart. I had a weak relationship with my classmates. Because the bullies harassed me, the good ones kept their distance from me, lest they be subjected to the same torture. In religion class, students were separated by religion. Teachers always thought me a Christian student at the beginning of the school year because of my name. I would smile, although embarrassed, among the whispers of the students. At this stage of my life, I made up a lie to justify my name: October War... Bar Lev Line... my dad the fighter whose Christian friend Daniel became a martyr while defending him. That lie used to leave a good impression on teachers and students alike, though one of my classmates corrected me once, saying, without being heard by any of our Christian classmates: "It is not right to call the Christian who died in the war a 'martyr' even if he was on our side. Martyrdom is only for those who are fighting for God, and all Christians will go to Hell because they are non-believers."

I did not dare to discuss. But I was shocked with the idea that Zio Roberto and Zia Kiara would not go to Heaven. I always imagined Heaven to be like Antoniades Park.[10] My mother and brother were waiting for me, between the trees and flowers, along with Zio Roberto, Zia Kiara, Nanny Attiyat, my father, and his always smiling orange Volkswagen.

Heaven in my imagination was full of warmth, love, and life. My mother was there now and of course she would open the doors for me. My twin brother was waiting for me there to play our postponed games. But Hell was not related to the afterlife; it was right there in school with all the innuendo, singing, and bullies — those keeping their distance and those making fun of my name, recalling the image of Farag when talking about my father. That is why I transferred a lot between schools. I was so happy when my father got fed up with my quarrels and complaints and decided that, after my preparatory stage, I would join the British secondary stage, an education system that did not require me to go to school or spend three years in the secondary stage. I studied my curriculum at home and private lessons were available when needed. At the end of each semester, I would go to the British Cultural Centre on Sultan Hussein Street to take my exams.

---

[10] A very famous park in Alexandria.

When the time came to choose my university studies, it was a done deal. My proficiency in both Arabic and English was equivalent to that in Demotic, hieroglyphics, and the Coptic and Greek scripts. My great passion for ancient monuments was far beyond an officer's suit or a doctor's stethoscope, which filled the dreams of many children.

University was a new world that cut the cord between me and the mysterious yet familiar world of my dad. Before, my life had been like an oasis with limited space, few people, a slow pace, and nothing bothering me except for the night raids that brought knocks to our door from time to time. But university life introduced me to a lot of people. Their noise bothered me. I stumbled behind their footsteps, and stuttered during conversations. Shyness was a thin, transparent curtain hiding my feelings from others; we would see each other, we would talk, but we did not shake hands and our shoulders would not rub.

The confusion about my name and identity chased me even in the university halls to the faculty prayer room in the basement under the hall. Nanny Attiyat always advised me not to miss any prayers and not to follow the habits of my dad, who barely performed the Friday prayer. He would do it once, then forget it several Fridays in a row… A bearded fellow usually led the prayers, then the students gathered around him in a circle; he used to lecture them about the meaning of some parts of the Quran or the Holy Hadith. Their meeting was simple and familiar, which is what attracted me. Sheikh Hosny came from a village from the El Behira Governorate. He resided in university student housing, was in his last year studying Arabic, and his devout voice reading the Quran attracted hearts and feelings. His clean socks had a hole that showed his toes, but Sheikh Hosny was not ashamed of that hole. On the contrary, it gave him enormous power as his humility was fortified by confidence. He stopped me once after the lecture and told me, "Brother Daniel… I know we do not choose our names, but God has forbidden us to imitate the non-believers, or to consider them as leaders. So, we should not be named after their names in the first place."

His deep voice and his self-confidence confused me. I tried to tell him my made-up story about the Bar Lev Line and the October War, but it did not impress him. He interrupted me, saying, "I know we do not choose our names. May God forgive your father for the unintended sin he made. Maybe you can fix this issue. You can officially change your name. The best names are the ones that thank or worship God. From now on, I will call you Abd El Hamid."[11]

Abd El Hamid Mohamed Abd El Razak... The name was a little bit strange to me, but the voice of Sheikh Hosny enchanted me. I accepted the name and planted it inside my heart as part of my identity.

That night, I told my father about my intentions and asked him to accompany me to the Civil Registry Office to officially change my name. He did not reject my request, but I saw a cloud passing across his blue eyes. He told me, with unexpected calmness, that he would do what I asked for, but only after I gave myself time to think about my decision.

The next day, I was surprised to find my father standing beside me in the prayer room of the faculty. Our shoulders touched each other as we prayed. Then he sat with Sheikh Hosny who appeared uneasy while watching my father's sparkling firm blue eyes — eyes that I never got used to. Sheikh Hosny welcomed the prestigious university professor, trying to hide his embarrassment with a smile. He hid the hole in his socks by covering one foot with another, while the other members of the brotherhood looked on curiously. My father said, "You have a nice voice, Sheikh Hosny, and you read the Quran quite well. My son Daniel praises your knowledge and your behaviour."

Hosny, surprised with this praise, smiled thankfully and started to praise my traits and attitude as well.

---

[11] Servant of God

"But what you said, Sheikh Hosny, about how the name *Daniel* is forbidden and that it must be changed, shows that you ignore the fundamental principles of the religion."

Sheikh Hosny was shocked; trying to maintain his smile, he said, "I did not mean anything bad, Professor. I only told brother Daniel the opinions of the sheikhs on this matter. Islam tells us not to use the names of non-Muslims. It is up to him to choose. I only wish to correct as many wrongs as I can. My guidance depends totally on God; I have put my trust in Him. To Him I have totally submitted."

"Do you know anything about the origin of the name *Daniel*, Brother Hosny? Do you know anything about Prophet Daniel's mosque?"

Everyone who lived in Alexandria, especially its university students, certainly knew the location of Prophet Daniel's mosque in Alexandria. Opposite the mosque wall there was a popular market for used books that students frequently visited, looking for references or old university books at low prices.

"I know, Professor, the grace of Prophet Daniel mentioned in the Torah. Islam teaches us to respect all the prophets prior to our messenger Mohamed, peace be upon him…"

"Did not I tell you that you are ignorant? Do you think that Prophet Daniel is the one who is buried in this mosque?"

"The common people believed so. That's why they named the mosque as such," Hosny answered in a faint voice

"But what you do not know is that Sheikh Mohamed Ibn Daniel Al Mosuly is the one who is buried in this mosque. He was one of the Al Shafi'i scholars in the eighth-century AD, a jurist scholar who came to Alexandria from Mosul, lived here, and studied in its mosque until he died in 810. The question now is: why did this great scholar never change his name if it was forbidden?"

The discussion only took a few moments; Sheikh Hosny looked like a small chick facing a hawk. I had never seen my father like this before. His pure blue eyes were full of lightning storms. His quiet and soft voice was sharp like a sword. The difference in their intellect and the logical evidence was clear between the shallow and the deep, the empty and the loaded. Sheikh Hosny tried to withdraw with his dignity intact, but he had been so completely humiliated in front of his followers that it wasn't possible.

I accompanied my father to his car on his way out. I did not want to go back to the faculty to meet the eyes of the brothers. My father told me he would come with me to start the procedure of changing my name by the end of the week if I still wanted to do so and that it would be my responsibility during the coming days to make up my mind. I did not say anything then, but I had already decided that I would not change my name.

When we were in front of the small orange car, my father's eyes regained their pure look. He told me in his quiet, familiar voice, "Son, beware of those who go to extreme prohibition and deprive themselves and others of God's mercy. Always remember that man has failed the test of divine obedience even when religion was only 'Do not eat from this tree.' All that was forbidden was an apple in a heaven that was full of other fruits. However, man fell into the trap of the prohibited. God's mercy is greater than those narrow-minded people; they love to forbid and search in the ancient texts. God is there in your mind and conscience. Obey them and you will obey God. Respect them and you will deserve God's mercy."

What happened in the next months made me stay away from the brothers forever. Sheikh Hosny disappeared, along with the bearded students that frequently went to the faculty's prayer room. We knew that they were arrested because they belonged to a Jihadist organization. This was announced in the newspapers. The weirdest thing that was said among my colleagues was that Sheikh Hosny himself was an agent for the state security and that he wrote regular reports on those who had extreme ideology within the college. I never knew the truth, but Sheikh Hosny came back to the college a few weeks later. Some of the brothers came back as well, while others disappeared forever. The dread around this topic prevented me from even following the conversations between my colleagues or the whispers of what had happened to them. My dad's history with dawn visitors and the memories of the catastrophic death of my brother pushed me far away from anything related to politics or in any way intersecting with the horrifying words of the state security.

That's why, after many years, I graduated from the university and became an assistant teacher holding a master's degree while waiting for the scholarship to get my PhD from London. I panicked when the chief of the university guards called me in my office, asking me to meet Haj Abd El Latif at 9:00 a.m. at the state security building on Pharos Street. The chief of guards felt the panic in my voice, so he attempted to calm me by saying, "Do not worry, Professor; it is just a small procedure to complete the scholarship papers."

I knew that all university scholarships and promotions in the governmental institutions, and even the medical treatment abroad paid by the country, were controlled by the state security, which was involved in everything. But this did not prevent me from asking about the details, without getting an answer.

"What is important is to not tell anyone at all about the meeting."

The chief of guards stressed this point which I buried in a deep well, where the echo repeated in a silent rhythm. I had no one to tell except my father. He was definitely the last person I wanted to know, although I knew he was the best person to tell me the details of the upcoming meeting: what I should say, what I should wear, how to greet and handle the hand-shaking. His long experience with dawn visitors and his thick file made him the most able to explain the meeting's details even before it started.

That evening, I went to bed early to escape his regard. I did not sleep. I heard my father's steps coming into my room more than once to check on me, so I pretended to be sleeping. This was probably the first time in my life I lied to him, and I did this without even uttering a word.

In the early morning, I was standing in front of the intimidating building one hour prior to the meeting. I walked a little bit. I bought a pack of cookies and a newspaper from a kiosk. I sat in a small coffee shop two streets away from the building. Morning rituals were happening all around me in the streets with many eyes looking at me. I tried to make myself busy, looking at the sports page in the newspaper.

After some time, I looked at my watch. My elbow hit the cup of the tea; it fell on the ground and broke. Drops of tea fell on my shirt, so I became preoccupied with cleaning them off. When the waiter calmly came to clean the glass from the ground, I felt that he was smiling on the inside. Who knows? Maybe he was observing my actions. Maybe he was going to write a security report about my confusing behaviour, or maybe he knew from experience that I was waiting for an appointment in the fearful building.

At 8:55 a.m., I entered the building which occupies a prestigious villa with a quiet European style. I asked at the information desk about Abd El Latif Bek. I left my national ID and my mobile phone. A scrawny detective with a rural accent came to me (he did not look at all like the image of Detective Farag, an image that still haunted me from my school years). He asked me, "Are you here for Haj Abd El Latif?"

He did not wait for my answer. He walked, and I followed, through the building's corridors. We went up two floors then into a small room that seemed unused, with only one wooden chair and an old-fashioned metal desk that no one had sat on for decades. He asked me to wait. I waited for four hours. I did not leave my chair; I did not dare to take one step outside the room he left me in. Every second I expected Detective Farag to enter the room.

By the time I left the room, I had memorized all that had been published in the newspaper, even the advertisements. I had also memorized the pattern of the stones that made up the floor: one black slab for every two white ones. I spent my last night with Alex, my twin brother, on a similar floor, freezing under a smelly blanket that was wet with the silent tears of my mother.

The creaking of the door broke the boredom of the prolonged waiting and the cold of the memories. Led yet again by the scrawny detective, we walked through a long corridor then stopped in front of one of the offices. He knocked and then gestured for me to enter. I entered the room trembling. I found an old man with a strong bone structure behind a black wooden desk. He stood up to shake hands with me and apologized for keeping me waiting so long.

He started talking to me in a friendly way and praised my good manners and academic prowess. He asked me about my opinion of the dean and the reason for his stubbornness towards me. My dry throat became a little bit lubricated after I took small sips of the lemonade that was brought in for me by the scrawny detective. I started to babble about the university and my PhD which I needed to prepare for, and the rude way in which the dean was treating me.

"Why didn't your father change his old dilapidated car after becoming a millionaire?"

I was surprised by the question, which changed the course of the conversation. One of the old buildings that my father inherited which was located in the Cleopatra district had fallen into disuse but he had still managed to sell it for a huge amount of money. I could not stop myself from smiling. In spite of the fact that my father never suffered from any financial problems thanks to this building that guaranteed a reasonable fixed income for us, the title of "millionaire" contradicted my father's simple lifestyle and the fact that he did not care about money. Even this huge amount he did not think of investing in any way or putting in the bank, or at the very least changing his car from the 1970s model. However, he had bought a piece of land in Karmooz, the local district, and started the procedures of establishing a cultural and service centre for the children of underserved, poor areas.

"Your father is really a kind man. Personally, I respect him very much and understand his academic and personal values. But unfortunately, he never thinks about his, or your own, wellbeing. The last heart surgery he had was a wake-up call. His heart can no longer bear the mistreatment. I hope you will do your duty to him; and, in return, you have my word that nothing bad will happen to him. No one will touch him or do anything to him."

Bit by bit, the details of the deal that Haj Abd El Latif was offering me started to become clear. My father's meetings with his friend were being repeated. They were working on establishing a group named *Enough* that gathered together different political movements to oppose President Mubarak and his son. All that was required from me was to provide weekly reports including the names of who was meeting with my father. I was surprised by the fact that Haj Abd El Latif described my father's friends the same way my mother used to: "The idiots party."

To spy on my father... I did not utter the words but it seemed like they were clearly written on my forehead. This made Haj Abd El Latif laugh. He said, "Do not think that I want you to spy on your father. Your manners and mine prevent me from asking that. Do not think that you are giving us information that we do not already know. You might be astonished that a lot of the group members are already presenting us daily reports. It is only that I want to help you and your father. I want to give you the opportunity to get the scholarship you deserve, and which you have been kept from, due to your father's thick file. I want your father to not have to be bothered by us anymore, so that his health doesn't bear the burden of our men's visits and of his detention for days or weeks at a time. I promise you that your cooperation will keep him completely safe no matter what happens."

I left Haj Abd El Latif's office with a dry throat, an empty mind, and a confused memory of what had transpired. I remember I somehow objected to what he said and that I nervously refused his offer. But his smile when he said goodbye meant that somehow, I had agreed to do what he told me.

Four months later, I was saying goodbye to my father. I cried on his shoulder while avoiding his eyes. I flew to London where, after a few days, I took off my glasses and wore for the first time in my life dark contact lenses to escape from the blue eyes and their silent reproach.

· · · · ·

The Fourth Voyage

Cyprus Island, 1269

From one land to another... from one sea to another... days and seasons passed. The pirates took over our ship in the middle of the sea. It was not a big fight. The sailors surrendered quickly, leaving the ship to its fate. Twenty men came down from the three invading ships and took all the weapons from the sailors and the passengers before locking them inside the ship. But they did not search the passengers thoroughly; I realized later that Hassan El Musly managed to hide his curved dagger, just as I had managed to save my father's golden ring that was hidden in my undergarments. I asked El Musly about our destiny; he said they were going to take us to the island of Cyprus, which is ruled by the Venetians and the Hospitaller Knights. They are the enemies of the people of Genoa and regularly plunder each other. We would remain in Cyprus as prisoners until one of the Venetian ships fell into the hands of the people of Genoa. They would then exchange prisoners and ships — either that or the dealers of Genoa would succeed in paying ransom for the goods and passengers who were on our ship.

But when we arrived at Cyprus, the Hospitaller Knights received us dressed in armour. Their chief was called Cardinal.

They had a young king who did not live among them, but lived in the Franks' land. He owned the throne of Jerusalem even though the land was in the grip of the Egyptian Sultan. But the Hospitallers had pledged themselves decades ago to go back, to take over the land and kill all the Muslims there.

The knights divided the passengers and sailors into groups. They put the merchants of Genoa and the captain of the ship into the prison of the castle. They put the Teuton and Slav sailors to work on their ships, and they put me and Hassan with the land slaves. Hassan told me, "The Hospitaller Knights refuse to enslave Christians, even if there is enmity between them. They treat them as captives waiting to be ransomed, while the Arabs, Muslims, Turks, and Persians who fall into their hands are either killed or enslaved in the vineyards and olive orchards. We are lucky they are in need of our efforts; it spared our necks."

Mixed-coloured people had become slaves of Cyprus farms: black, dark brown, chestnut, and blonde, most of whom had been captured in the campaigns of the knights on the harbours of Egypt and Levant; or kidnapped by the pirates while they were travelling by sea for trade. Some of them had the same looks of the Frank people: white, blond, and tall with a huge body, like the first one I met. His name was Hance and he was a heathen, one of the northern refugee sailors. Their land sprouted ice and fire. One day in their country was equivalent to months in our country, which was strange, but they said it explained the size of their bodies and the whiteness of their faces.

The oldest slave, the most prestigious and the one who had been there the longest time, was an old Egyptian man called Youness. He was taciturn, a hard worker, and an expert in agriculture and the secrets of the land. He divided the work among the rest of the slaves and kept for himself the tasks that required the most effort. He worked as ten men do, and ate less than a small child. He sang long prayers at night in the manner of Egyptian Copts.

He sang hymns from their holy book in a language that was only understood by those from which it came.

I asked him why he was among the slaves, as I knew that the Hospitaller Knights did not enslave Christians. He became completely silent. But the next day, he saw me writing on my papyrus, so he respected me. He respected science and people who could read and write. He started to talk and asked me about my stock of papyrus, so I gave him some of it. He thankfully accepted the gift, but warned me, "Knights should not see me writing. They believe that the Arabic language writes only heresy and magic. They even chastised one of the Frank teachers because he dared use Arabic numbers instead of Roman numerals, justifying that it makes calculations easier. They said he was addressing the devil and using witchcraft and sorcery to conspire against the Holy Spirit."

"How can we escape? We cannot spend our lives here under the yoke of slavery; plowing and harvesting." Hassan El Musly had appeared and asked this passionately; he was dying to accomplish a mission that I knew nothing of.

With a stern look, Youness the Egyptian replied, "The island talks about runaway slaves; it is surrounded by the sea on all sides. The knights do not bother themselves by guarding their human cattle because they know that running away is a guaranteed loss."

Hassan swallowed the answer silently. Agitated, he brought a small leather bag out of his clothing. Opening it, he cut with his fingernail an infinitesimally small portion of black substance. He put it in a jar that already contained burning embers and, with a hollow stick, mixed it around before inhaling the smoke contained inside the jar. Very rapidly, he forgot the depression of imprisonment and smiled, breaking into songs that no one understood except him. After a little while, he fell asleep. He didn't move until the morning, when he woke up and told us, "I spent my night in Heaven."

There was a smell of poppy oil in the black substance. It is a plant that comes from the lands of the Persians; it helps with pain relief and the treatment of headaches and migraines. I heard that smoking it in the way Hassan had brought the mind into a state of euphoria and serenity for a period of time, which is why it is not forbidden by many Islamic religious men. Others believe it has the same effect as wine.

The following night, Hassan El Musly caught the fever again. I could not reach my medical herbs; all I had around me were lemon and willow trees. But rubbing his chest with lemon and chewing willow bark was not enough. He became worse, babbling at night words that I could not understand, something about the next Mehdi[12] in the last decade and the Maulana, who ordered him to open the eternal gate in Rome. He repeated the same phrase over and over again:

"I heard and obeyed Maulana, heard and obeyed my sheikh. I will sacrifice my blood and soul to fulfill your orders."

I asked Youness the Egyptian for help. If I could reach my luggage and herbs, I could probably save him. Youness went away for a while and came back with a small bag, a little larger than his hand, made of gazelle leather. It contained a dry, dark powder. He brought out some of it and put it in Hassan's mouth, who spat it out while mumbling what sounded like spells in a strange rhythmic language.

Youness the Egyptian observed the hallucinations of Hassan and frowned. He asked me about my friend; I told him the circumstances by which I knew him. He told me that he did not feel good about him.

"The Franks do not allow Eastern people to get on ships going to their country except for a good reason. Even the traders

---

[12] The prophesied redeemer of Islam who will rule the world before the Day of Judgment and rid the world of evil.

put up some obstacles to keep their share of the profit. Your friend is not a merchant carrying goods, so there must be a dark secret in his journey. There is blood waiting to be spilled by his curved dagger."

He said all this without stopping his treatment with his wondrous powder and strange spells, which I knew were secrets of the old Pharaohs. Astonishingly, his ministrations succeeded in saving El Musly; he was cured from his fever within a few days.

The long nights had people talking, so we started exchanging stories and news of the roads and our trips. It was bizarre; when Youness the Egyptian heard my story, he cried and told me that he knew my father, Prince Pitar; and my uncle, Louis IX, King of the Franks. He also might have heard of my mother. He remembered a beautiful Egyptian prisoner that Prince Pitar kept for himself. The knights had talked about how she used an Arabic magic spell on him to make him stop believing in the Christian religion and kidnap him to a Muslim camp.

I asked him why he was in the Frank camp in Damietta. I thought they had taken him as a prisoner, like what happened with my mother, but he said that he went to them by his own free will.

He had dedicated himself to God in the Qalamoun Monastery, but he was shocked that the bishop had devoted himself to gold and dinars. Religion was being bought and sold. Simon the Magician was gathering followers everywhere, so Youness went to meet the Pope in Alexandria; he was surprised to know that the corruption had actually started with him, that Simony had become a competitive religion for Christianity, and that gold had become a cross that was raised everywhere. The good reputation of the kind pope vanished and Youness' prophecy came true. The Pope's chair in Alexandria was empty for twenty years until a crook named Dawood Bin Laqlaq took the position.

The pious monks and clergy that were not corrupted by money gathered to discharge him six years after his inauguration, but by then, Youness the Egyptian had lost his faith in everything. When the Franks' campaign came to Damietta, Youness was affected by what he had heard about King Louis' asceticism and religion. They said he did not wear anything except rough wool, and kneeled for his prayers until his knees ulcerated. Thus, Youness the Egyptian insisted on meeting King Louis, so that maybe he would find the right path to God through him.

"I was immigrating to God's path." That's what Youness the Egyptian said, crying, when remembering what happened while he was invading the Franks' camp in Damietta. He asked to meet the saint king, who met him with great hospitality, and who made Youness a close confidante. The king made Youness his counsellor and showed him all the circumstances and details of the country. Youness the Egyptian overlooked the knights' brutality and their thirst for bloodshed under the name of the cross. They were like lost sheep that must return to the right path, since the shepherd is good and directs them. When the Frank soldiers were defeated and the king was captured by the Mamluks, there was nothing left to make Youness want to go back to Egypt. His fellow monks denied and rejected him, saying that he was contaminated by treason and had sold his country to the enemy. He got onto the Franks' ships and travelled with them to their faraway lands. He went from being a close counsellor to a runaway follower and a humiliated refugee. His rank kept falling as the ship sped farther away from the shores of Egypt. He was told by the knights that he should be baptized again to wash himself from the Eastern infidelity and to return to the proper religious path. He should kneel in front of the Roman pope, kiss his holy ring, and curse those who disobeyed his authority, those who clung to Eastern heresy and its church. Youness refused; thus, the knights dropped him off in Cyprus. They sold him as a slave to the Hospitallers for a few dirhams. Mockingly, they told him that his price would be part of the ransom for King Louis IX, who was imprisoned in Mansoura under the swords of the Mamluks.

I asked him again the same question he had avoided when I first met him, "Don't the Hospitallers forbid themselves from enslaving Christians who are following the Cross?"

This time, he replied with sorrow, "They say so, but they do not do it. They put the Cross on their shields but have removed it from their hearts. They consider all Eastern people to be the same, with no difference between those who follow Prophet Mohamed or those who follow Christ. They consider us barbarians, and our land that of atheism, although Christ himself and his messengers came from there, blessed by the Lord. I did not refuse to become a slave, nor did I rebel against it. I accepted my lot with contentment. It is a punishment I deserve for the redemption of my sin. Whenever I miss Egypt's palm trees and the Nile, I remember the sin of going with the procession of the enemies..."

Hassan El Musly joined our conversation then. His face cramped when he heard Youness the Egyptian talking about Simony and the selling of the religious positions by the church. He said with obvious anger, "They are all vicious: the pope in Rome, the caliphate in Baghdad... those who are trading the words of God are everywhere. When the land rids itself of them, this would be the announcement of that promised hour. When the Mehdi returns and sits on his awaited throne, he will fill the world with justice instead of tyranny. Blessed is he who paves the way under the feet of the awaited Mehdi. Blessed is he who reduces the waiting time. A few years ago, the caliphate in Baghdad was defeated by the Tatars. The Egyptian sultan tried to nominate a new Caliph from amongst the Abbassy princes, but groups from the Nizari sect ambushed the candidate and killed him to leave the caliph's chair empty. It is true that the Egyptian sultan tried again to choose a caliph and kept him beside him in the castle of

Cairo. But the daggers of the assassins13 would definitely reach him. Sheikh Hassan Al Sabah's fellows are capable of executing the mission and bringing the Mehdi's time closer. Vacating the throne of the caliph of the Muslims alone would not be enough. The throne of the pope in Rome should also be emptied from those who rape the Word of the Lord. The pope's throne has been empty for two years now, and the Frank kings are fighting. Every one of them wants to nominate a pope from among his own followers. Even if one of them were to succeed, the newcomer would not stay for long; the daggers of the assassins are capable of killing him anywhere he goes."

Hassan El Musly shuddered while talking. His understanding of what he was saying was more than just a firm belief. The handle of his dagger was barely hidden in his clothes... I looked to Youness the Egyptian to find him listening silently, his eyes calm and tranquil, his lips mouthing a Demotic hymn:

---

[13] Assassins or Alhacahah are an Ismaili Nizari sect, separated from the Fatimids in the eleventh-century AD, which calls for the ruling of Nizar Al Mustafa Li Din Allah and his descendants. It was famous between the eleventh- and the thirteenth-century AD. Their basic strongholds were in Persia and Syria, after some of them migrated from Iran. Hassan Al Sabbah founded the sect: he made the fortress of Alamut in Persia the centre to disseminate his call. Strengthening the pillars of his state became an intense feud with the two caliphates, Abbasid and Fatimid.

The military strategy of Hchachen relied on assassinations carried out by 'fedayeen' who did not care about death in order to achieve their goal. Where these Fedayeen brought terror into the hearts of the rulers and princes hostile to them, they were able to assassinate several very important figures in that time (for example the minister Seljuk Nizam Al Mulk and the Abbasid Caliph, the other Abbasid Caliph Al Rashid, and the King of Jerusalem Conrad of Monferrato).

Hulagu ended this state by a huge massacre and burning of the Ismaili castles and offices. Shortly after they would fall down in Syria after losing their political independence by the Zahir Baybars in 1273.

The way of the Lord does not need
To travel
nor migrate
Luggage, followers nor path companions
The way of the Lord
One carries it in his heart
If the heat is lit by faith, it is open for all paths and roads...
I did not realize in my whole trip
From east to west
Across the wide sea
Desert, forest and foreign lands
That I take my real own way, it does not take me...
I walk with it, I do not walk in it...
In Cyprus fields, under the swords of the knights and the yoke of slavery
I finally realized my freedom...
Under my skin and between my veins and at the core of my soul lies my freedom
The path is hiding from the eyes of the researchers
Waiting for the arrivals

It didn't look like much, but translating this short hymn took hours. Though I tried to preserve some of the rhyming in the translation, the demotic text carried a special magic and musical rhythm that was difficult to translate.

I had just finished putting the final touches on the translation when Professor Geovany invited me for a special meeting that would include Doctor Abd El Hussein El Jaafary and myself. Professor Geovany was very much interested in the character of Hassan El Musly who was mentioned in Ibn Al Bitar manuscripts. Some of his characteristics matched those of another person mentioned in documents that goes back to the thirteenth century. Kept in the Vatican Library, these documents talk about a follower from the Hachacheen group who infiltrated Rome trying to kill the pope.

Everyone who studied European history knows that the origin of the Italian word *assassinio* and the English *assassin*, which means to kill or to murder, goes back to the Middle Ages. It was inspired by the Arabic word *hashasheen* which was the name of a group of Shia Nizari who were famous for the assassinations they carried out. Some researchers think that the origin of the word is *hassaneen*, which means followers of Hassan Al Sabah, the leader of the Nizari, who were known later as the Hashasheen (the Assassins).

"It would be great if our research could find the missing link in the Vatican Library. The Hashasheen's attempts to kill the pope is mentioned in some documents. The manuscripts we have now will help rewrite this part of thirteenth-century history."

That's how Professor Geovany started his talk, only to be interrupted by Professor Hussein El Jaafary:

"Professor Geovany, I do not think that true scientific research language should use the term *Hashasheen*; we know that using this word to refer to the Shia group who follows Hassan Al Sabah is mostly myth rather than the truth."

What Professor Abd El Hussein El Jaafari said was true to an extent, despite the spreading of the idea that Sheikh Hassan Al Sabah, the leader of the Nizari, made his followers inhale cannabis smoke to become unconscious. After this, he would order slaves to carry them to a place in his fortified castle which he called *Heaven* (a fruitful garden full of wine and beautiful girls) where he convinced his men while they were under the ecstasy of the cannabis that they were dead... and that they went to Heaven to see with their own eyes what was waiting for them when they obeyed their leader. When they were sober again, he would convince them that he had brought them back to life. This myth, though very famous, had no scientific or historical evidence. But even historians who were contemporaries of Hassan Al Sabah — who were against him and described his followers as mystic and atheist — did not call them *Hashasheen*, whose initial meaning was 'people addicted to inhaling cannabis.' They did mention this myth which was peddled by the fertile European imagination, attempting to justify the high boldness that characterized the Fedayeen of this group while they carried out suicidal assassination missions.

"It is not a myth, Professor Jaafary. You know that Marco Polo told the story of the Hashasheen in his trips and mentioned that he saw Al Mawut Castle and the gardens of Heaven with his own eyes," Professor Geovany said.

"Professor Geovany, you know that Marco Polo was born in 1259, while Al Mawut castle and the Nazari country was destroyed by Hulagu two years before… Also, Marco Polo did not start his trips until twenty years after that date. Subsequently, it is impossible that he was an eyewitness who narrated these scenes… What is more logical is that he copied the stories and myths he heard, like any tourist who quickly visits a place and writes about it," Professor Jaafary replied sharply.

"Aha!" came Professor Geovany's victorious shout. "You say that he copied stories he heard, which means that the story was common among the contemporaries of the Nizari group… and that the idea of inhaling cannabis smoke and preparing suicide missions in that way (which certainly could have been an exaggeration) probably have their root in some measure of truth."

I stepped into the conversation for the first time, trying to calm the debate, "Whatever the case may be, certainly we cannot deal with the story of the Hashasheen as historical fact, but at the same time we cannot assert that it is completely false. That's probably what Professor Geovany meant."

It seems that my contribution was ineffective, because Professor Abd El Hussein El Jaafari burned with anger, saying, "So far, there is no evidence that the Hassan El Musly who is mentioned in the Ibn Al Bitar manuscript belongs to the Shia Nizari group by any means. Is it because he smells of cannabis and carries a dagger that he must be on a suicide mission? Is that what you two want to prove? That all Shiites are murderers? That all Muslims are terrorists? I reject this awful racism!"

An overwhelming anger exploded over the facial features of Professor Geovany. Racism contradicts everything I know about him. In addition, whenever the word *racism* is mentioned in Western scientific forums, it is as strong as a swear word. For a few seconds, it seemed like the flood of anger between the Iraqi and the Italian, both masters of anger, would sweep away any attempt to cling to reason. But the verbal sparring calmed down after a while. Fortunately, the meeting included only the three of us; maybe if there had been more people, it would have been problematic, leaving at the end scientists exchanging blame and apologies. Instead, a cautious composure returned to the room.

"Let's put this nonsense aside, Professor. The Hashasheen are clearly mentioned in the manuscript you are studying. Ibn Al Bitar mentioned that word twice so far. He even pointed clearly to the fact that it is probably them who killed Caliph Abbasid who was sent to Baghdad by Zahir Baybars," Professor Geovany said in a tone that conveyed he clearly wanted to be rational and calm.

"But there is no evidence that the Hassan El Musly mentioned in the manuscript belongs to any doctrine or specific group," Professor Jaafary replied.

"Exactly. No evidence, but as mentioned, anything is possible," Professor Geovany said.

I tried to contribute once more but before I could open my mouth to speak, Professor Geovany stopped me: "We are scientists, Professor. We search for facts, not sayings, not subjective opinions. All that I am asking is to keep looking. We have clear gaps in the character of Hassan El Musly that I hope we can fill in by the contents of the manuscripts we already have. I contacted the Vatican museum and Professor Marco Gazelli, the secretary of the manuscripts in the old museum, and he will send us a report about the translation of some of the Latin manuscripts kept there. They date back to the thirteenth century. We will have the report in a few days. I want us to use it as a guide while we are trying to collect the pieces of the puzzle related to this unique cache we are investigating."

The meeting came to an end soon after. I did not know why I was so worried about Ibn Al Bitar and his companions. Professor Gazelli was known in academic circles as having investigated the most famous documents of the thirteenth-century Inquisition, and he had gained his fame from a documentary episode that he presented on the National Geographic channel entitled "Torture Machines." All would make sense.

'THE RULING MILITARY JUNTA ISSUES AN AMNESTY ORDER FOR TERRORISTS AND EXTREMISTS.'

'ABBOUD AL ZOMO IS RELEASED; HE IS THE LAST ONE ACCUSED OF THE ASSASSINATION OF SADAT.'

'MORE THAN 3000 MEMBERS OF THE JIHAD ORGANIZATION AND THE ISLAMIC GROUP BENEFITED FROM THE AMNESTY AND RETURNED TO CAIRO AFTER MANY YEARS SPENT IN AFGHANISTAN AND PAKISTAN.'

SELECTED EGYPTIAN NEWSPAPER HEADLINES,
MARCH 2011

Spring of Alexandria

Alexandria, 15th March 2011

I spent a month and a few days in Rome, all of it accompanied by Ibn Al Bitar, Youness the Egyptian, and the team trying to understand them. But I received an email from Egypt that changed my plans to stay until the mystery had been solved. I asked Maria the following morning to book a flight to Alexandria, then I told Professor Geovany that I had to be away for one week. I was being urgently summoned by Alexandria University administration to finalize the paperwork regarding my vacation which I wasn't able to complete, as I had left during the revolution. At the same time, I needed to consult certain experts in Coptic history about the manuscripts of Youness the Egyptian. Professor Geovany warned me about exposing any secrets related to the cache. The protocol of archaeological research imposes a strict system about discoveries until the official institution responsible for the research announces it.

Professor Geovany smiled while saying goodbye to me, wished me a pleasant trip, and winked for reasons I didn't understand while Maria brought me my ticket.

"I allowed myself to reserve two tickets, as you might need your personal assistant on this trip," she said in such a charming way that it aroused a storm of pleasure inside of me. As much as I had missed Alexandria during the last few days, I had been feeling upset at having to leave Maria's smiling eyes and cheerful spirit. I could not hide my happiness.

"Great! You are going to enjoy the most beautiful city in the world!"

"I wanted my first visit to Alexandria to be a vacation, but Professor Geovany insisted that it should be a business trip."

From the sky, Alexandria was clear. Streets seemed washed by the rains of yesterday, and the sun was glowing behind a thin layer of clouds which made it look more prestigious and mysterious, much like the silk face cover of a Turkish dancer in an Ottoman harem.

The secret behind the beauty of the rainbow is the variety of colours it contains. If the sun had one colour, life would lose its meaning. Most likely the secret behind the success of the Spring Revolution in Egypt is that Tahrir Square and other squares all around Egypt were open to all colours and believers at the same time, which made the rainbow irresistible. Maybe Alexandria's prestige has always been due to the rainbow it has always contained. Colours, denominations, religions, and different races have lived for many centuries in one city, with none of them becoming dominant over the other, and each one preserving its special identity and colour. Fifty years ago, one third of the inhabitants of the city were Europeans and foreigners, and society became a mixture of different cultures. Even when they left the city, they left behind their colours in the rainbow of the city: be it in the layout of the streets, the architecture of the buildings, the names of the districts, or in Alexandrian slang.

My moment of praise for the beauty of Alexandria was interrupted by Maria's impatient sigh. The eastern port arch seen from the window of a plane made it look like a mermaid resting by her eternal lover.

Two hours later, when she was on the balcony of her room in Cecil hotel overlooking the eastern harbour, Maria sighed once more while facing the serene sea. The gracious March breeze was playing with her dark hair. I couldn't resist the opportunity, and what happened next. The universe melted in our first kiss, filled with the salty smell of the sea and the euphoria of discovery.

I decided to reserve a room for myself in the same hotel, since my apartment was far away from both here and from the university. My father's apartment in the Al Azarita district had been closed for a long time and it would need a lot of effort and time to be cleaned... Or at least that's what I convinced myself, using so-called rational reasons to follow my heart and stay in the room next to Maria's.

I loved Alexandria. I had travelled the world and had yet to find a prettier place. Even wonderful Rome, decorated with Roman swords, Renaissance marble, the Pope's crosses, and gold from all ages... I laughed when anyone compared it to Alexandria, considering the historical conflict between the two.

My love of Alexandria was related to the place, not its inhabitants. I didn't have friends or family that could bring me back here, or even an old teenage love, the nostalgic memories of which would make me want to return. I had no relationship with any one of the inhabitants, but the entire population as a whole carried the spirit of the city and my love for her.

The smiling taxi driver who dropped me off at Alexandria University was chatting and filled with optimism. He proudly talked about how he had defended his neighbourhood during the revolution and of his young neighbour who was martyred during the Friday of Anger. On the front window of the taxi was a picture of children next to the monument of the Unknown Soldier in Mansheya Square. He told me his children insisted that they should participate in the revolution and they had accompanied him several times as he joined various protests calling for Mubarak to step down. He decided to quit smoking after February 11th, telling himself that the country would change and that he himself should change as well. He was jumping from one topic to another with enthusiasm, like a happy little bird hopping from branch to branch among different types of trees. After ten minutes, I couldn't stop myself from smiling.

I counted more than seven different topics he moved onto without noticing that I did not participate actively in the conversation; I only nodded my head from time to time.

At the gate of the university, I found a large sign that announced: "The flowers that blossomed in Egypt's gardens." Pictures of university students who had died during the January revolution were under it. I knew one of them: he had been my student two years ago, an activist of the group called 'We Are All Khaled Saied.' He had called, months before the revolution, for protests against the killing of an Alexandrian young man by two policemen. I felt deep sorrow when I saw the photo of my smiling student. I stood there for a few moments praying for him, the other martyrs, and my father.

Inside the university's management office, vacation procedures were not so complicated. I could have completed them by sending a fax as I was used to doing. I could not understand why I had been summoned from Rome to finalize routine paperwork. I gave one of the office guys my file to finalize the procedures for me, and waited for him in the cafeteria. I purchased a cappuccino. It felt like a punishment compared to the taste of its Italian counterpart, still lingering on my tongue.

Students were gathered everywhere. Their victorious enthusiasm was full of optimism and had a lot of space for tolerance of contradictory visions. Changing the world had become a possibility.

"Yesterday, we broke into the State Security secret building."

"Another edifice of fear and oppression fell under the feet of the protestors!"

"We did not only break the fear barrier but also the barrier of depression as well. Mubarak did not rule us with a strict security like Saddam Hussein in Iraq, for example, but he succeeded in suffocating our dreams and ambitions. He convinced Egyptians that this is the best we can have. When there is no ambition, people yield and become submissive to the president despite his poor qualifications."

A skinny brunette girl was talking to a group of students as if she were giving a speech. The scarf on her shoulders was colourful, indicating her leftist political direction. She was not more than twenty years old, almost a child rather than a young lady. I could not prevent myself from smiling as I caught myself with what exactly I was suffering from in the academic community of the *old people*. Despite all that I had achieved as a world-renowned academic, I would be thirty-eight years old next October. This was why the title Young Professor, which clung to me, had become a way to mock and ridicule me among the university professors in Egypt as much as it was a show of appreciation in the academic communities abroad.

I took another sip of the hideous cappuccino, deep in thought. I was twenty years older than this young lady and her colleagues who were the fuel of the revolution, but when I heard them talking, I felt that the title Young Professor seemed unfamiliar and strange. Youth is enthusiasm, cheerfulness, positive energy, irreverence towards the laws of the universe, and being fully confident that you can change it. With my thirty-eight years, I was not a young man at all, but then again, I probably never had been. On the contrary, it was my father who had the youthful spirit in his heart even when he was about to turn sixty.

I was so immersed in my thoughts that I did not notice the voices of the students quieting down. I only saw four of them walking towards me. The girl with the Palestinian shawl was one of them, and she greeted me, "Professor Daniel, welcome back. Thank God you arrived safely."

I knew that her name was Yomna, that she was a student in the Faculty of Arts, and that she was the head of the cultural activity in the centre of Alexander, dedicated to developing the community which was established by my father in the district of Karmooz. She talked with great appreciation about the importance of the centre in raising awareness among youth, informing them about democracy and its mechanisms, and serving the community of the poor districts around the centre. She said that my father's spirit still existed among the new generation of youth who were concerned with public affairs. They were considering holding a seminar to honour the national and political figures who had preached the revolution for many years and died before seeing it happen. In addition to my father there was Professor Ahmed Abd Allah Rozza, political scientist and leader of student activities in the seventies; Doctor Abdul Wahab Meseiri, thinker and former General Secretary of the Kifaya movement; Ahmed Nabil Al Helaly, human rights lawyer; and Yusuf Chahine, film director.

She was interrupted at this point by one of the other students objecting to the addition of the name of Yusuf Chahine, referring to rumours about his personal life. Another colleague angrily described Ahmed Nabil Al Helaly as an atheist communist; a long thin young man replied to this:

"Watch your language when you are talking about the leftists' saint, that noble man who defended everyone and is respected by everyone. Ask your sheikhs about him. They will tell you how he suffered from harassment and abuse for defending them in front of the courts in the eighties. He disagreed with them in opinion and approach, but he was ready to protect their freedom and their right to express it with his life."

The debate intensified about the figures of art and politics who suffered persecution and lack of appreciation in the era of Mubarak because of their attitudes and because they were defending certain principles. Soon, voices became louder as supporters and opponents started clashing.

The administrative assistant caught my attention then; he had finished his work, but, as he leaned in to give me some papers, he got distracted for a moment by the fighting students. He then asked me to pass by the office of the head of university security, who wanted to see me about something important. I walked to his office, feeling uncomfortable. I had buried that feeling in my memories tomb long ago… but the head of security met me with a silly smile then he got a name out of that tomb and said, "Haj Abd El Latif sends his greetings."

Many years had passed since my one and only meeting with Haj Abd El Latif in the Security State Office. The head of university security told me that Haj Abd El Latif wanted me to pass by his place. He gave me a downtown address and said that he would be there every day until 3:00 p.m.

"He just wants to have a cup of coffee with you. Try to spare him some time during these coming days."

As I left the university's administration building, the salty sea breeze touched my lips. I looked at my watch. It was eleven thirty in the morning. It was still early. I did not want to be late for Maria whom I had left alone in the hotel. But I also wanted to be done with the meeting with Haj Abd El Latif, so that it would not be a pending issue. This time, however, I wasn't fearful or anxious. I just felt uncomfortable and disgusted. I waved to a taxi, and gave the taxi driver the address on Safia Zaghloul Street.

The taxi stopped in front of a classy old building in a commercial street full of shops and cinemas. I got out and passed the crowded entrance, my eyes scanning the various signs. I reached the sign for the Global Navigation Agencies Company and noted the office number. I walked to the old wooden lift which appeared to be from the thirties. I got off on the third floor to find a newly renovated apartment with marble walls and huge wooden doors decorated in gold. I went inside to find a good-looking young lady at reception. I gave her my name and seconds later, I was received by Haj Abd El Latif in his office with the enthusiasm one reserved for an old friend.

Years had not changed anything about his looks except for the addition of some grey hair. He had the same gentle elegance, sharp look, and dominant yet quiet tone. I remembered that I never knew his military rank; I never heard anyone calling him *pasha,* which is usually used by police officers. He requested a lemonade for me but I told him I preferred coffee for now. He smiled and asked the young lady to bring him a coffee as well.

"Congratulation on the new office. It seems you left public service and were welcomed into the private."

I was trying to gain control of the conversation, but he laughed and did not comment. Instead, he got a file out of his desk and put it in front of me, saying, "Here you are, Doctor, so that you know I always keep my word."

My heart sank when I opened the file containing the reports I had written with my own hands about my father and his visitors. I could not take my eyes away from the file, although there was one letter in particular that I could not read.

"You know, Professor, considering the current chaotic state of the country, the breaking into the headquarters of state security, and the seizure of countless documents by protesters... I was worried that these papers might get into the hands of irresponsible people that would cause you deep embarrassment."

I did not reply. I felt in his tone of voice a hidden threat that I did not like, but I knew that there was a lot of truth behind what he was saying. During the past couple of days, activists had displayed on social media a lot of documents that had been taken from state security headquarters. Despite repeated assurances that state security officers had shredded important documents and transferred all originals to safe places far away from the reach of the protestors, this did not prevent the spread of a large number of documents of which the credibility was difficult to check, and of which the existence was sufficient to fill talk shows and fuel gossip.

I was playing with the file. I kept closing and opening it again and again, giving myself a cut on my smallest finger with its plastic cover. I placed my finger in my mouth to suck on the wound, thinking about how it felt like I was holding papers made of metaphorical thorns.

I coldly thanked Haj Abd El Latif, and then we talked a little bit about what was happening in the country and its political future until it was polite enough for me to bid farewell. But before I could leave, he asked me, "Why did you not activate your Egyptian mobile line until now? I hope you will activate it. Someone will call you very soon."

I tried to ask him about the nature of that mysterious call, but the thorns in my hand were pushing me to leave. Back on the street, I did not look for a taxi, walking instead past Safia Zaghloul Street directly to El Raml Station Square, where the turquoise colour of the sea mixes with the blue sky. Whenever I took a step, the horizon appeared more clearly between the buildings and the hustle. After less than ten minutes, I was on the Corniche in front of Cecil Hotel. I climbed the huge cubic stones that separated the Corniche from the waves of the sea. I sat on a stone near the water, took out the papers from the file, and started tearing them into tiny pieces before tossing them to melt into the water. I then stretched my hand into the water to wash my injured finger, hissing at the sting of the salt. Gradually, the soothing of the cold water overcame the sting of salt in the open wound.

The Fifth Voyage

Cyprus Island, November 1269

The sea overflowed with blood.

Every day, the waves brought a corpse that had been snapped by an unknown fangs and mysterious claws: a villager from the town of Lefkosia, sheep and cows torn apart, the daughter of one of the fishermen, and finally, Hans the Pagan. I saw his deformed corpse with my own eyes after it was spit out by the sea. He had been cut apart, making people wonder of the power that succeeded in conquering this giant titan. Prayers filled the churches, and the villagers said that this was done by the dragon which lived in the Troodos Mountains inside his well-known cave. It had been sleeping since the days of the Christ but recently had been awakened by God to burn the Earth after it had become overshadowed by corruption. Judgment Day is close; the Pope's chair in Rome has been vacant for two years, and the Frank kings and princes continue fighting.

The cardinal stood at Sunday prayers reciting from the Book of Revelation:

"Then I stood on the sand of the sea, saw a beast coming up out of the sea, having seven heads and ten horns; upon his horns ten crowns; upon his heads the name of blasphemy. The beast which I saw was like a tiger, his legs like the legs of a bear, his mouth like the mouth of a lion. The dragon gave him his power, his throne, and a great authority."

People started crying, bidding each other goodbye, retrieving their hidden gold and giving it to the Church. The knights wanted to fight the dragon and kill it, but the cardinal stopped them.

"It is written that if the dragon appeared, it would not be defeated by armies nor weapons, and that only one man who has true faith can kill it or send it back to slumber and postpone God's judgment."

I asked Youness the Egyptian about the location of the Troodos mountains and the cave of the dragon. He told me it was far away, on the other side of the island. I asked him how the dragon came here every day to catch his prey without being seen by anyone. He rebuffed me and asked me to remain silent, saying that if anyone heard me asking this question, the sea would throw my deformed body out the next day. I did not understand but the warning in his eyes made me obey him and keep silent.

Word spread in the village that the cardinal would face the dragon himself. He built a grand wooden statue in the square depicting a dragon form as described by the Book of Revelation. In the heads, he made flares of fire instead of a mouth. He put sheep's meat in its belly and started to train hunting dogs to approach it and bite the meat in the stomach without being afraid of the fire. People gathered in the square, full of hope and horror, praising and praying to God. Ships passing by carried news of the dragon; some of them came back with news about prayers held in churches throughout the Frank countries, asking God to postpone his judgment and to support the cardinal of Cyprus against the dragon of the final days.

On departure night, the cardinal collected his hunting dogs and ten of his slaves. I was one of them along with Youness the Egyptian and Hassan El Musly. He made his loyal and faithful knights guard us, then he ordered us to bring six hundred and sixty-six sheep while heading to the Troodos Mountains.

The trip took us one day and night. When we arrived at the foothills overlooking the edge of the sea, he ordered us to wait to let the herd of sheep graze freely without reining in their roaming. He asked his knights to build a huge wooden cross out of cedar trees and raise it high up to the sky. He then slipped an arrow out of his quiver and sent it flying toward the mountain. He ordered us not to go beyond the arrow no matter what happened. The cardinal spent the night praying, then he took off at first light of dawn with a sword and a spear, carrying his iron armour decorated with the sign of the Cross. On his arm was tied a purple badge given to him by the pope years ago, when he was appointed as a cardinal. The hounds followed him.

. . . . .

Once I activated my Egyptian mobile line as Haj Abd El Latif had asked me to, a message notification popped up. I opened it; it was signed by Sheikh Hatem Kamal El Din. It contained a nice greeting and a request to call him.

Sheikh Hatem Kamal El Din? Astonished, I re-read the message from the famous television preacher, the owner of the Believers' Channel... I had never watched that channel, but many parts of Sheikh Hatem's programs and fatwas were circulated by activists on YouTube. They raised a lot of fuss because of the witty way Sheikh Hatem handled serious and debatable topics, which made a lot of his admirers dislike him and his views with a sacred aura, calling him Mawlana.

But the most famous video I recently saw of him was a collection of old programs where he forbids protesting against President Mubarak, criminalizing the calling for demonstrations and sit-ins, which he sees as disobeying the ruler whom God ordered us to obey. In another recent video, uploaded after the success of the revolution, he is attacking Mubarak and his regime and heralding the victory of Islam over an unjust ruler and corrupt regime. Activists gave the title "Hypocrisy of Sheikh Hatem, State Security" to this video.

"What does Sheikh Hatem want from me? Is that the phone call that Haj Abd El Latif asked me to activate my line for?" I wondered while pressing the call button. After a few rings, the rough voice of a young man speaking Classical Arabic with a rural accent answered.

"You want Mawlana? Who are you? ... Ah... One moment."

After a moment of silence, I was talking with the famous Mawlana. He sounded very welcoming, as if he, too, had known me for a long time. He said that he was in Alexandria and would like to meet me about something important.

"I will be in the Al Qae'ed Ibrahim Mosque to deliver a speech after Al Eshaa prayer. What do you think; can you attend?"

"Excuse me, Mr. Sheikh…"

I felt strange saying "Mr. Sheikh," but I did not know the title that I should use… Should I say "Master Sheikh" or "Sir Sheikh?" I did not feel like saying the word "Mawlana…" I continued, saying, "I have foreign guests whom I cannot leave. Maybe you can visit me in the hotel for coffee? I am staying at the Cecil Hotel, not far from the Al Qae'ed Ibrahim Mosque."

"You and your guests are most welcome, Professor, for dinner tonight. I will wait for you at 9:00 p.m., in Al Madina El Monawara restaurant, next to the Library of Alexandria, close to the hotel and to the mosque."

Sheikh Hatem insisted on the invitation, and refused to accept any apology from me, so I reluctantly agreed. I told Maria. She was happy; I had left her alone most of the day at the hotel. I did not want to leave her at night as well and spend it in an unexpected meeting… she surprised me when we were going out by wearing a cotton T-shirt with "EGYPT JAN25" written on it in English. I knew she had bought it when I was out at Al Raml Station Square, in front of the main gate of the hotel, where some of the protestors were still there for a reason that was not known to a lot of people.

At 8:00 p.m., we went outside to walk on the Corniche. Maria was impressed with all the details of the city. The prestigious statue at the centre of Al Raml Station Square, facing the sea, caught her attention. She asked me about it. I explained that it was for Saad Zaghloul, the national leader who led a revolt against the British occupation in 1919.

"It is clear that your history is full of revolutions. Why is the media then saying that the January Revolution is an exceptional incident for a nation that has not rebelled since the pharaohs?"

I smiled at her remark. I wanted to comment but felt it would lead into a lecture in history and politics that I did not have the energy for at that moment. Instead, I jumped the fence of the Corniche to embrace the sea breeze.

"In my childhood, fishing in this spot was my favourite hobby. The house where I was raised is not far from here. I will take you for a visit."

Maria jumped up cheerfully to walk with me on the stone fence separating the Corniche's pavement and the waves of the sea. She asked me why I was in a bad mood upon my return earlier that day from the university. I did not answer. She respected my silence and did not insist.

Soon she was sighing at the impressive sight of Al Qae'ed Ibrahim Mosque, which we were walking by. She asked me about its history. I laughed, and said, "Al Qae'ed Ibrahim Mosque is one of a few Italian monuments in Alexandria. Your people built it!"

She was astonished, so I explained how the mosque was built by an Italian engineer by the name of Mario Rossy in the 1940s. He had been living in Egypt since the beginning of the twentieth century and had embraced Islam without changing his Italian name. He worked in the engineering department in the Ministry of Endowments and was fascinated by the Mamluk architecture. So, he built this mosque in a modern architectural style, combining elements of Mamluk art while forfeiting others, such as the corridors and open courtyards.

"So, do you mean that this mosque is considered an 'Italian monument' in Alexandria?" she said with a smile. I replied with the enthusiasm of an archaeological scientist:

"Rather it is an example of different cultures meeting. Tomorrow I will take you to the cemeteries of Kom el Shoqafa to see a unique statue that combines Pharaonic and Greek artistic influences. We might have time in Cairo to visit the Coptic museum. You will find inscriptions from the early Christian era discovered in a tomb in Alexandria as well as the boat of the god Ra in which the soul sails to the other world, with the sign of the Cross on it — idolatry and Christianity in the same piece of art. This cultural and civilizational mixture is the spirit of Alexandria, the pulsating heart of which hasn't changed through the ages."

At 8:45 p.m., we were entering the vast restaurant. Its two floors were located in a modern building beside the Library of Alexandria and faced the sea. Its wide entrance made of marble and glass gave the people sitting inside a clear view of the Corniche. The golden flashy decorative signs were clear in a way similar to the busy baroque inscriptions: all bustle without taste or identity.

I asked one of the waiters for Sheikh Hatem. He smiled cheerfully and told me that Mawlana had invited me and my friend to wait for him in his private suite. The owner of the restaurant came in person to welcome the guests of Mawlana. He quickly took us to an upper floor to a wide round table facing the sea. Our table private and relatively isolated from the rest of the restaurant which was full of people.

After a while, there was hoopla in the restaurant during the entrance of Sheikh Hatem and his companions who looked as if they had just come from Osama bin Laden's den in Tora Bora. The owner of the restaurant welcomed him at the external gate. The crew of waiters mixed with his companions at his grand entrance. He was a giant with a big belly wearing a suit under a cloak decorated with golden weaves; his long white beard was coloured with henna.

He smiled widely, leaving everyone with the mysterious impact of simplicity mixed with fear.

The companions of Sheikh Hatem sat at the next table, while he sat with Maria and me in a very warm, welcoming manner. He asked me about Maria, and I explained that she was my colleague, an Italian archeological scientist. He looked at her, smiling, while asking me:

"Does she speak Arabic?"

"No."

"I thought she was your Filipino servant."

I did not like his rude comment. I felt upset, but he did not notice. He was looking at her face while saying his racist joke, but her neutral reaction convinced him that she did not understand Arabic. He then greeted her in English, "Welcome to Egypt!"

The way he said it reminded me of a street salesman who sells souvenirs in the tourist areas. Maria replied to his greeting in a very polite manner.

The owner of the restaurant came personally with a waiter holding a tray filled with all kinds of salads and appetizers. He asked us what we wanted to have. Maria ordered grilled steak, and so did I, despite Sheikh Hatem insisting that I should try the oven-cooked lamb, the restaurant's specialty.

I wanted time to pass quickly, as I was not feeling comfortable about the situation. I made sure to chat with Maria every now and then so as not to let her feel neglected in a meeting she had nothing to do with.

Sheikh Hatem's fingers sank in the stacked pieces of meat over a mountain of rice and nuts. He started talking with a mouth full of food, "I used to wonder about your name. Were it not for the fact that Haj Abd El Latif assured me that you are a good Muslim, I would have thought that you had — God forbid — converted to Christianity."

"Haj Abd El Latif?" I replied, shocked.

"A kind man and a good brother. He highly praises you. He considers you as one of the faithful young men to their country and religion, in addition to your highly respected position in international forums. What's better than invading them in their own place with science, and forcing them to give us a space and a position in their academic institutions."

Sheikh Hatem was talking in short bursts, interrupted by chewing and swallowing, or by the owner of the restaurant checking that everything was ok, or trying to convince Maria to try certain pieces of meat, which she politely declined each time.

When he finished eating and the waiters had removed the leftovers, Sheikh Hatem leaned back in his wide chair and sipped his tea. It felt like he was about to broach the topic that had brought me here in the first place. He leaned towards me and said, "The Believers' channel will launch a campaign to correct the concepts of secularism, liberalism, and communism for the youth, which invaded their minds with a lot of talk against the true religion. We want you, Brother Daniel, to be our guest to talk about your father. He did not pray, right?"

I was surprised by the question. I did not even reply, as it seemed like Sheikh Hatem was not waiting for my answer before continuing, "May God forgive him for the sin of tempting the youth who were fascinated by the ideas of communism and secularism because of him. I am sure he had good intentions, but… Do you know that the centre he established in Karmooz district under the umbrella of 'serving the community' teaches music but not the Quran? They hold seminars about the liberation of women yet do not hold lectures about religion, the only way to fix society!"

"Do you mean the *Alexander* centre?"

"Even the name of the centre has a Christian echo to it which is not related to our religion and culture, as if the names of the noble companions of Prophet Mohamed ran out, and we could not find anyone except a Christian infidel king name to name the centre after."

Certainly, the most provocative thing for a professor specialized in history and monuments is mentioning the wrong historical information… for the first time I found myself being urged to object. The words flew out of my mouth, tinged with sarcasm, "A Christian king? Alexander the Great died three centuries before the emergence of Christianity!"

"Only God is the Great. There is no difference whether Alexander was a pagan or Christian. All of them will go to Hell on Judgment Day."

He said it in a real grumpy manner, unhappy about being caught making a mistake. I did not want to have a long debate with him, which would take too much time, so instead, I tried to close the conversation, "Anyway, you probably know, Sheikh Hatem, that I have no authority on the Alexander Centre. It's managed by a board of trustees, and my father coordinated their framework before his death."

"It does not matter. It is enough that you denounce the activities of the centre in our interview. Leave the rest to us and our followers; they are capable of adjusting to the middle path. May God accept this action: it would become an ongoing charity for your father, rather than keeping the centre as a sin which would torment him in his grave. It is enough that he is tormented for having chosen a Christian name for his son."

I was incensed; I could not bear the continuous offences on the memory of my father by a man who gave himself the right to hold the keys of Heaven and Hell. I had tried to end the meeting with some dignity, but he had gone too far in talking about the religious beliefs of my dad, calling him an infidel liberal communist. I did not understand the logic behind linking these three adjectives together, but I could not overcome my feeling of disgust. I found myself yelling at him things that blew up his prestige among his Kandarian followers, who were listening from a distance at my raising voice and seeing how their leader was looking angrily at me.

Seconds later, I burst out of the restaurant, followed by Maria. The sea breeze calmed me down a little and, after a few moments, I was even able to smile. Maria noticed my smile and said, sarcastically, "Now you are smiling! I thought for a second you were going to fight him with your bare hands!"

"Can you imagine this was the first time in my life I have known the feeling of becoming angry? I do not remember if I have ever been angry before…"

She looked at me with loving eyes and gently wiped a tear from my cheek. I did not know it had slipped from my eyes…

It was not only the feeling of anger that I was experiencing for the first time in my life, but also another fresh feeling that cleaned my emotions. It was the very first time in my life that I was capable of expressing my feelings and talking about them out loud.

"Maria… You are the closest person to my heart in this world."

"It seems like I can go back to thank that rude man," she said with another smile while gently squeezing my hand before continuing, "What did he tell you that made you so romantic?"

I told her part of the conversation I had had with the sheikh. When I came to the part related to my name, she did not understand why it had hit so hard, so I told her the real story… the one that I sometimes forgot because I had been hiding it behind the fabricated story of the Bar-Lev line.

"My father, may God have mercy on him, was an archaeologist obsessed with finding Alexander the Great's tomb. He spent his life excavating for the cemetery in different places. By the time we were born, he was excavating a cemetery under a monumental mosque in Alexandria named the Mosque of the Prophet Daniel… the archaeological studies he conducted supported the theory that the tomb of Alexander the Great was under that mosque. He decided, optimistically, to name the twin boys that were born at that time Daniel and Alexander."

"You have a twin brother, Danny? Amazing! You never told me that before!"

"My twin brother Alex died a long time ago, when we were children."

My face became gloomy, so Maria changed the subject and asked me about my relationship with my father.

"Obviously, you were close."

"To a certain extent. Until the end of my twentieth year, I had no relatives or friends, so my father was everything to me."

I said this while looking into her eyes, absorbing her cheerful spirit and the love of life. A crazy idea crossed my mind, and I acted on it immediately: I grabbed her hand, turned away from the sea, and jogged across the Corniche towards the Al Azarita district.

"Would you like to meet him?"

"Who?"

"My father."

She looked at me, puzzled, while putting effort into keeping up with me. A few moments later, we were on a quiet street parallel to the Corniche. I pointed towards an old building.

"I was raised in this building. Our apartment was on the second floor. I inherited the whole thing from my father."

When I passed the entrance, I felt her surprise at not going in. I smiled and, a moment later, understanding dawned in her eyes as we entered a large parking garage under the building. I greeted Mahmoud, the old man taking care of the parking garage, and, after a short conversation about how everything was going, I walked into the garage to find the small orange Volkswagen: clean, shining and always ready for a ride, thanks to Mahmoud's gentle care and my strict instructions.

"This car was the companion of my childhood and part of my father's soul."

"It's great!"

"It is a 1970 model, almost new when my father went to Cairo to participate in the Tahrir demonstrations in 1972. It kept waiting for him for many long months in front of Cairo University until he came out of prison after everything was finished. How about a ride in the most beautiful city in the world with the most beautiful car in the world, and…"

I opened the car door, leaned for her to come in, and then finished my sentence:

"...with the most beautiful girl in the world?"

I heard her laughter while I closed the door and ran around the car to sit behind the steering wheel.

"Thanks for the nice compliment. So, you think that I am old-fashioned, like the Volkswagen?"

"Well, no. I see you as the most precious treasure on Earth. Priceless things in life are called so simply because they derive their value from the value of life itself."

Then I laughed while continuing the joke, saying, "Which means your value is equivalent to the value of the tomb of Alexander the Great to my father."

She laughed while pretending to be angry, but she couldn't pull it off. She hit my shoulder with her soft fist in mock rage. I laugh right along, seemingly for the first time in my life.

We drove the small orange car through the lively streets of Alexandria. The curfew was officially still in effect, but the joyous city defied it and the tanks, as it had during the days of the revolution. We drove along the sea, then entered the classic, dignified, and prestigious downtown streets. We crossed Suez Canal Street towards the police station where the effects of the fire that took place by the hands of the demonstrators on the Friday of Anger were still visible.

I circled around the Alexander the Great statue to go back to Fouad Street. As if introducing my beloved one to my lover, I explained to Maria the details of the city which I knew like the back of my hand: cinemas, mosques, Jewish temples, and churches dedicated to so many Europeans and Eastern deities... The art of the Mediterranean architecture that lived in the buildings, the Ptolemaic city planning, its main streets lying deep under the streets of the twenty-first century... the Royal Neighbourhood, the Hype Stadium, Canopic Road under the road of freedom... The tomb of Alexander was overlooking the road, as mentioned by the historian Strabon, who witnessed the end of the Ptolemaic state and the beginning of the Roman era. At Prophet Daniel Street, I slowed the car down until I stopped and I explained the history of the old mosque, whose name was always a burden on me.

At the end of the night, we found ourselves at El Raml Station Square. Under the statue of Saad Zaghloul were a group of young people thrilled by their sit-in. I could not think of a specific reason for their sit-in, but they were fighting the cold by singing the same songs that I used to listen to my father and his friends sing:

> O Mother Egypt, you are gorgeous,
> Dressed up in dress and scarf
> Time has grown old, and you are young
> Time is going away, you are coming
> Walking above difficulties
> Hundreds of nights passed
> Your endurance and smile
> Are still the same

Young people sang out loud with voices roughened by their all-day cheering and the cold of the night. Warmth covered the area under the statue of Saad Zaghloul, who stared eternally at the darkness of the sea. Maria started clapping her hands to the rhythm. I noticed, among the youth, Yomna: the student who welcomed me this morning in the university. My entrance with Maria increased the enthusiasm among the group, and my fresh and loud voice sang over their exhausted ones:

> O Mother Egypt, you are a ship
> No matter how high the sea was
> Your peasants become your sailors
> The just calls the wind; it calms down
> The one who is holding the rudder is a craftsman
> The one who is holding the paddle is a champion

We became zealous. A young man jumped on the pedestal and pretended to be a sailor looking at the sea; his voice was raised over the chorus, singing:

> The one watching over the mast
> Is watching all that is coming and going

We repeated after him enthusiastically, along with the exhausted voices:

> You will ride the high wave
> O Egypt you reach the shore safely
> Youthful and gorgeous

Some nights just never end. They last for years, travelling across ages, leaving a silky spectrum of memories, like the taste of a mysterious smell that fills the air whenever it is recalled. When we passed the gate of the hotel with dawn smiling down at us from the intersection of the sea and the sky, Maria and I were sure that this night will be remembered forever.

> Oh, if only I knew that with this night I was saying goodbye to the Alexandria that I know...
> Oh, if only I knew that I would never be here again,
> My eyes would not be able to enjoy looking at it once more...
> Oh, if only I knew...

Parenthesis

By Maria Satriano

When I am assigned to collect the writings of Professor Daniel Abd El Razak, I try to honestly convey what he wrote. But in this exact moment, while remembering our first night in Alexandria, my emotions rebel and refuse to deal with the texts neutrally from an academic, cold perspective. Tears flow out of my eyes, preventing me from being able to see the rest of the documents without stopping for a moment to think about the destiny of this huge love which has dissolves in my soul since the very first moment I met him, if not before.

Women have their own intuition. Sometimes we can look into the eyes of a man for the first time and we know somehow that we have met the one.

This is what happened with Danny. My feelings were clear from the beginning, even when our feelings started to grow quickly and turn into a deep relationship. My friends, colleagues, and family have warned me not to rush without giving it time to mature. They think rationally, calculating givens and results. But emotions always have something else to say.

Deep inside, I always feel that I am racing with time, undertaking an unknown trip that I know nothing about. My man is with me now, but he might fade away any second.

The coming days prove me right. I have never regretted rushing into love and dissolving into the soul of my beloved. I shall be his companion on every trip, even if there is darkness, witches, or thieves. It is enough for me just to be with him all the time. It is enough for both of us to have the same destiny.

The Sixth Voyage

Cyprus Island, 1269

The cardinal was away for a day and night. The next morning, we heard barking dogs approaching. We saw a tangle of dust rise up in the air at the foot of the mountain where it meets water. As they approached, we saw the cardinal's horse running quickly past the huge wooden cross towards us. We hurried to meet him; when we came closer, we saw the cardinal's body, still wearing his iron shield, hung over the back of the horse without any sign of life. But when we stopped the horse and started bringing the cardinal down, he moved. In a very weak voice, he told us that the dragon had been slain. The knights cheered in celebration, took him, and bandaged his wounds. After a while, they blew their horns celebrating the victory. The cardinal had succeeded in defeating the monster. He killed the dragon and its body fell into the sea. Saint Gorgeous had been resurrected in the body of the cardinal. The famous symbol of the *Romanian Hero* stabbing the dragon symbolizes the new miracle which took place by the leader of the Hospitallers.

The news of the victory reached the fort before us. Peasants and fishermen held up drawings of for Saint Gorgeous, while cheering for the living saint whose faith had saved humanity from vanishing. God responded to the prayer and gave human beings additional time to repent of their sins.

"There is still some time before the world ends. The dragon has been defeated by a man of faith; he postponed God's will." That is how the peasants narrated the story which spread quickly, confirmed by the saints and the priests who narrated a lot of other stories about the details of the cardinal's victory over the dragon. Some of them said he did not raise a weapon in its face, but he looked into its eyes and drew a cross, then the dragon knelt down before throwing itself into the sea. Others confirmed that a bolt of lightning hit the dragon before it fell into the sea, and still others shared different details about the battle. Others shared the story of the bloody battle in which the cardinal and the dragon fought, which explained the cardinal's injuries. When the dragon was about to win, the cardinal knelt down to spend his last moments praying; an angel appeared and hit the dragon with his wing, cut off three heads, then stabbed the dragon with a spear. This made the dragon fall into the water with a huge noise, leaving no trace.

The dragon would disappear in the unknown caves for one thousand years until its heads would regenerate. God would then send it to other people misled by Satan and deserving to be punished.

Strangely, all these stories preceded our victorious cortege which was leading the sheep. I wondered how they knew what we did not see, though we were miles and days ahead of them.

When we reached the fort, all the knights, inhabitants of the villages and cities, and slaves of the land came out singing and praying. The cardinal stepped off the horse and stood before them, seemingly recovered from his wounds. Everyone knelt in prayer to thank God. The voice of the cardinal echoed as he recited:

"Let us thank the Maker of the good things, the merciful, the Father of our Lord, our God and Saviour Jesus Christ ... because He has covered, helped, saved, accepted, had mercy, strengthened, and brought us to this hour... so also ask Him in this holy day in which He protected us from the beast and extended our days on Earth, may we repent of our sins; may He make all the days of our lives in peace."

The cardinal's voice trembled with a humility which ignited the crowd. A voice among the crowd proclaimed the sanctity of the cardinal who was chosen by the Lord to defeat the beast mentioned in the Book of Revelation. Others cheered, calling the cardinal to fill the pope's chair, which has been empty for years. The cardinal spoke modestly, advising the crowd to quit talking about positions and leave it to the will of God Almighty. But at the end of the celebration, when everyone went to sleep after a long exhausting day, all were convinced that the cardinal was the envoy of the providence to the Christian world to fill the pope's chair, which has been vacant for the longest time since Saint Peter set the rock, the church of God, on Earth.

I did not realize that these events would free us from the pangs of slavery. The cardinal, who wanted his victory to be spread across the Franks' countries, gave his orders to set all the Frank prisoners, imprisoned in the fort, free. He returned the stolen ships of Genoa to its people as a reconciliation with Christ. In the outpouring of generosity and tolerance, the captain of our ship requested to have Hassan El Musly and I back. He told the cardinal that we were in his custody. He had signed a deed at the Port of Damietta promising to preserve our safety, and to take us back to the port within one year, carrying the share of the Sultan from the profit of our trade. The cardinal agreed and the cavalry removed the yoke of slavery. My goods, which were in the ship of the captain of Genoa, were restored to me.

Despite the happiness of having regained my freedom, I cried out of sadness for leaving Youness the Egyptian. Even Hassan El Musly's tough face and hard heart were softened. He tried to convince the captain of the ship to ask the cardinal to take Youness with us, but the captain refused. He said that he could only ask for the passengers of his ship; as for Youness, he is a slave owned by the Hospitallers, he could not talk about him with the cardinal.

"Do not cross the line in your demand, or you will provoke the cardinal's indignation and lose everything," the captain said to Hassan, warning him, and closing the discussion.

I wept while saying goodbye to kind-hearted Youness the Egyptian, but Hassan thought about it and planned something we knew nothing about. He secretly told me that he had paid a piece of gold to one of the sailors to let Youness escape with us and hide in the goods storage room. He would sneak by night to get on the ship with us. The knights would not realize he was missing until morning, when we would be far out at sea. I was so happy with the plan that I forgot to ask Hassan how he got this piece of gold while he was enslaved.

I ran happily to Youness, informing him of the news, but he was not happy. He cried while trying to overcome his longing to return to Egypt, because he knew of the danger behind this plan.

"You are putting yourselves in danger for my sake. If we are caught, the Hospitallers will not have mercy on us. They control the island with fear. Prisoners are not imprisoned in a cell with bars; instead, they imprison their souls with bars. That's why they insist on torturing any slave who tries to flee, even if he could make it to the sea. They have their ships and men in every harbour. No, I will not allow you to sacrifice yourselves."

He said this while hugging me gratefully. But Hassan refused, and said, "I owe you. You saved my life once, and this debt must be paid. It is a done deal. If I had to knock you out and carry you to the ship, so be it."

Time was running out. Father Youness finally yielded because of my insistence and Hassan's determination. Two hours before departure, the three of us were getting onto the ship covered by the darkness of the night and the intentional negligence of the sailor because of the piece of gold. The old man hid in the dark of the storage room, while I sat with Hassan on the deck listening to the sounds of the celebration that reached us from afar. The cardinal made sure he left a good impression on the leaving sailors; they would be his ambassadors all over Europe with the story of his victory over the dragon. He held a huge carnival, where the knights competed in the various games. Clowns spread laughter among the audience. The village people gathered around the grill fire at night. Wine hidden away in antique vaults was poured generously.

At dawn, the sails of the ship swelled with the favourable winds. Happy sailors were leaving the harbour which seemed like a ghost town. The noisy night left its aftereffects on the residents of the city and the surrounding villages. It was clear that the island would take longer than usual to shake off the euphoria of last night. Likely no one would notice the absence of Youness until midday. The wind and the waves might help us... We did not know that we were fleeing from God's destiny to God's destiny, and that sometimes the shackles of slavery are more merciful than the mazes of a free life.

Demotic Hymn

"They deceive you

Thus they say light is beautiful

And darkness is ugly

They deceive you

Light is not beautiful in itself

But it gives us the ability to see the beauty around us

They deceive you

They liken God to light

God is beautiful in Himself

His light does not reveal things

But His light inhabits things

Look at God inside you

Be beautiful

So that your soul can

Receive the light of the Lord, without showing its ugliness

Be worthy of this light"[14]

---

[14] Note that this hymn is incomplete. The papyrus is worn out and some ink has disappeared. The last two lines are dependent on restoration.

Back to Rome

Rome, April to September 2011

My lifestyle changed when I went back to Rome. Maria became my life. I left my room in the hotel and went to live with her in spite of the warning of Professor Geovany that mixing business and personal is inconvenient according to the traditions and regulations of academic work. But when he saw how my life was starting to be filled with happiness, he overlooked this administrative observation.

Professor Geovany asked me to settle in Rome. The Professor of Egyptology position at La Sapienza University was waiting to be filled. Professor Geovany nominated me to fill this position, and Maria was thrilled when I told her. We planned to spend some of the summer together in the south of Italy on the beautiful Amalfi coast, then head to the province of Satriano near Naples to meet her family.

"This is a very advanced step, Danny. Shouldn't you slow down a bit before taking it? Maria is a magnificent girl and you are like my nephew, but the few weeks or months you have spent together is not enough to assure a long-term relationship."

This advice was given to me by Professor Geovany and other colleagues when they heard about our summer plans. Maria was from the south of Italy, where, like the Japanese, they had a conservative culture and strictly follow traditions and family values. Going with her to meet her family meant that we were as good as engaged, and we would begin the official procedures. Actually, I felt comfortable about this idea despite all the warnings. She was from the south and so was I: how similar the south of Italy is to the customs and traditions, and even religions, of the south Mediterranean. Sometimes, when I dealt with people in Italy, I felt that the Mediterranean was narrower than the river Nile; and that Naples, Amalfi, Bernadette, and Palermo were just suburbs of Alexandria.

But that summer turned out completely different than what I had hoped for.

The Believers' Channel started a series of episodes attacking the symbols of different political views. The channel devoted two consecutive episodes to talking about my father. Sheikh Galal Al Barchoumy (the famous program presenter on the Believers' Channel) called my father a communist atheist. He brought various testimonies from people who said they knew him; they analyzed all his actions, assessed his views and positions, and they all concluded that he was an atheist who opposed and rejected religion. They even used my name to demonstrate their point of view.

"Have you ever seen a Muslim man who calls his son 'Daniel?'" Sheikh Galal Al Barchoumy asked in a heavy rural dialect after he received phone calls that insulted my father and all what he represented.

"Committing the sin of infidelity was not enough for that atheist man; he even fought Islam to the extent that he established a centre to spread Christianity and the principles of infidel Freemasonry. He was funded by foreign organizations who did not want any good for this country or for this religion. Of course, whoever sells himself to the Zionists will find huge amounts of money flowing over his head," Sheikh Barchoumy said on another day.

I watched a lot of videos on YouTube attacking my father. Sometimes I felt that whoever was making these videos only meant to be sarcastic; no one could have all these contradictory concepts, after all, could they? *Liberalism, communism, atheism, masonic, and Christian* all together… Even the simplest of minds understand that one cannot be both Christian and atheist at the same time.

But the redness in their eyes, the droplets that flew from their mouths as they spoke, the way they moved their hands, and their facial expressions and body language while listening to the phone calls made it clear that they believed all of it to be absolutely true.

Over the next few days, the number of videos of sheikhs insulting my father increased. Some news sites also reported that lawyers were raising a proclamation to the general attorney demanding to close the Alexander Centre for Community Development under the pretext that it was established with Zionist funds and carrying out dubious missions of preaching Christianity and Freemasonry. It also worked to corrupt society by teaching Satanic arts, music, and Western ideas that were not in line with the traditions of our Islamic society.

Then came the news about bearded men attacking the centre and burning parts of it down, beating young people who tried to defend it — including Yomna, that young lady with enormous energy who I met during my last visit to Alexandria. Activists published some videos on YouTube of her trying to defend the outer gate of the centre, bravely confronting the attackers, only to have one of them slap her so hard that she fell to the ground before being dragged by her feet away from the gate, while her attacker's colleagues stepped on parts of her body as they entered the centre. The video spread through social media eliciting both anger and sympathy. A women's organization conducted demonstrations to raise the slogan: "Women of Egypt are a red line." Demonstrators said that the failure to arrest the aggressors, despite the fact that their faces appeared clearly in the video, was unacceptable.

But the Believers' Channel continued its campaign:

> "If that girl had stayed in her home, she would have been dignified and untouched, as Islam says. What makes a girl put herself in that suspicious situation, to talk to men and confront them?"

Sheikh Galal Al Barchoumy said this on a TV show the day following the incident, then he continued in a tough rural accent that abandoned the prestigious classical Arabic he tried to uphold:

> "Would any man allow himself to be insulted by a woman? No way. In our village, if any girl were to cross the line, then she would deserve whatever happens to her. Of course, they removed the voice from the video they are spreading on the internet so that the dirty words the girl said would not be heard. Shame on them!"

The director then displayed the scene of the famous attack again, attempting to focus on Yomna's face as she yelled in the face of young intruders just moments before the dragging scene. The purity of the image diminished with zoom, as well as through distortion from being uploaded to YouTube; thus, the facial details turned into confusing coloured dots. But the voice of Sheikh Galal Al Barchoumy pursuing the scene said, "See how she talks to the young man? Muslim men have dignity and are not cold-blooded. In spite of how she is talking to him, he does not respond to her. See! See! He is just trying to get her out of the way, but she pretends to fall to the ground. I swear to God she is pretending."

. . . . .

One day I received a strange call from someone who introduced himself to me as Tariq Mamdouh, programmer of one of the talk show programs on a channel famous for supporting the civil state. He asked me to participate in the show through a phone call to exculpate the accusations of atheism being brought again my father. Tariq asked me cautiously, as if he wanted to be sure, "Of course, Professor Mohamed Abd El Razak was Muslim and believed... was he not?"

I was surprised by the question. Seconds later, when I hung up the phone, I did not exactly know what I was feeling. It was not anger, sadness, or even disgust... Bitterness?

The idea of defending my father's beliefs, to prove that he was a true Muslim, to count the prayers he prayed and the Quran lines he read, defending why he didn't go to Hajj...

"Do you not know that those who can but do not go for Hajj for five years become infidels?"

These were the questions with which the Believers Channel were chasing the minds of the people in Egypt as they destroyed my father's memory and scolded his grave like the dogs of the cemeteries.

"Why did all of this outrage against my father erupt now, five years after his death? Why did they snap his dead body, destroy his memory, and pollute his reputation, which has always been pure white?"

I asked these questions over a telephone call to a friend of my father and he said, "When the revolution took place in Egypt, most of the political activists carried out the civil, liberal, and leftist movements to which your father belonged. The religious parties and military rulers are now distorting the symbols of political activists who have practiced political action and demanded freedoms for decades."

"But why my father" I asked angrily.

"Your father was also keen to raise awareness even after his death. That is why he established a cultural centre for the development of society in a popular area. Military and religious men want to break the popularity of this symbol before the upcoming election."

I remembered what had happened in Alexandria few months before. Haj abd elatif, the high-ranking officer in the state security was the link between me and Sheikh Hatem. He had asked me to activate my mobile and to wait for his call and listen to what he would tell me. The goal was to use my father's reputation and give them a chance to control the centre of Alexander the Great, which was spreading awareness among young people. Awareness is the greatest enemy for both military rulers and clerics who aspire to power.

I lived a long time without anger, and probably without feelings too. I mean real feelings that had a taste. My feelings never had taste; they were all pale. There was a dark cave in my heart guarded by a dragon; all my secrets were hidden in these cold depths.

But something had changed since my last visit to Alexandria. As if the dragon had left the cave, it was now open to anyone. During my last trip to Alexandria, I had been touched for the first time by anger and love. For the first time in my life, I had explicitly expressed both: anger when I yelled at Sheikh Hatem, and love when I tasted Maria's lips. For the very first time, I found true, pure, and clear emotions imposing themselves on my behaviour and actions.

I had changed since my return to Rome. I had become hotheaded. I tasted fresh emotions, and then I expressed them clearly before others. My colleagues had noticed, with Professor Geovany telling me, "Something has changed about you… Your attitude and your appearance as well."

He meant not only the flicker of love in my eyes, but also the fresh and volatile emotions when dealing with my colleagues in different situations… as if there were gasoline in my blood. Professor Abd Al Hussein no longer dared to irritate me with his mysterious arrogant hints or words that had several implied meanings. He started to set limits in dealing with me after the huge anger he faced from me when he mocked the Egyptian revolution and called it an 'uprising of thugs.' It is firmly known in Western academic institutions that one is not allowed to despise any race, nation, or country. This was why our colleagues intervened to calm me down. They forced him to apologize publicly for what he had said.

And so when Tariq Mamdouh called me onto the famous talk show, I tried to cool down and stop that burning gasoline in my veins while talking objectively about my father, defending his religious beliefs and his cultural project. His dream was to establish a centre for social development in one of the local areas with the goal of spreading thought, culture, and awareness.

"My father considered Alexander the Great more than a king or a military commander. He believed that no matter how great the military victories, it was no more than just iron, blood, and gold. Genghis Khan and Timor Lank conquered lands exactly like Alexander, and they marched victorious with their armies like Alexander. But what really differentiated Alexander, a student of Aristotle, was how he led a movement in the world. He sought to mix civilizations, bring people together, and help them meet. For that reason, he respected the civilization of every country he opened, he understood the culture of the oppressed people, and he even accepted their gods. This is what made my father consider Alexander greater than just a military commander or king. If we considered human civilization as a religion or a creed, Alexander would rise to the rank of prophet."

The presenter tried to make me comment on what was taking place in Egypt: the process of democratization after the revolution, the constitution, the elections, demonstrations, and other details. I told him that, because I lived abroad, I could not express what was happening because I was far from the ground. I said that I certainly hoped that the democratic process would proceed and that people would be aware enough to choose wisely.

I ended the call feeling *satisfied*. But when I recalled the details of what I had said, I started going back and blaming myself for not saying one thing or another.

Maria laughed when she saw me recalling the details of the phone call on my way to the bedroom, absent-minded and mumbling. She hugged me from behind and leaned over to kiss my ear, whispering playfully, "Only married guys become insane to the extent that they talk to themselves. You still have a long time before you reach this stage."

The smell of her dark black hair filled my breath and its softness touched my right cheek gently. I smiled and turned towards her, kissed her, and apologized.

In the following days, there were unexpected reactions for my phone call. The Believers Channel continued its campaign against my father and his political and intellectual beliefs. Sheikh Galal Al Barchoumy used part of my phone call in his own TV program, an excerpt that had already been spread widely through social media. In this excerpt, I was defending the role of the Centre of Alexander the Great in spreading awareness and culture, saying, "My father wanted to establish a public service institution, a charity service centre like the hundreds of charity clinics and centres for memorizing the Quran that have been established by the good people in Alexandria. He considered the establishment of a centre that cultivates cultural awareness as a charitable deed for the sake of God. You can see that there are many charity clinics and centres for memorizing the Quran. However, only one institution teaches music, and few public libraries have, in their collections, the latest books to help youth taste the beauty of art in all its forms."

Sheikh Galal Al Barchoumy replied to this intentionally cropped part of my conversation in his tough rural dialect which he used whenever he wanted to attack someone harshly, "Oh my God! See the atheism! Is not he ashamed? He is upset that there are many centres for memorizing the Quran, he considers music equivalent to the verses of God! These are the licorice candies that tempt and corrupt the community, my brothers. Secularists, masons, and converts who want to extinguish the light of God with their mouths. God refuses extinguishing. He enlightens even if the non-believers hate that… If the secularists hate that… If the converts hate that… If the masons hate that…"

Sheikh Galal Al Barchoumy was waving his head right and left to the rhythm of his last words, his face turning red out of anger. At the bottom of the video which was posted on YouTube, the number of views exceeded a hundred thousand. Hundreds of comments glorified the jealousy of Sheikh Galal Al Barchoumy on Islam and cursed the converts and the non-believers who corrupt society. Of course, my father and I received a huge share of the curses and insults. Some of the commentators volunteered to confirm that I belonged to the group of the Copts of the Diaspora living in the corrupted West, and that I was ambushing Egypt and its Muslims.

I tried to stay away from this collective hysteria. I blamed myself for getting involved. My new life was beginning in Rome with passionate love and enthusiastic work. The summer trip to the south of Italy to meet Maria's family was enough to keep me from following everything that was happening in Egypt. I relaxed on the magical beach of Amalfi, the beauty of which was increased by the renewed vividness of Maria. Her family welcomed me in a kind manner. At the end of the visit, I saw Maria carrying a big black leather bag. I asked her about it; she smiled, and did not reply.

When we were back in Rome, she took out an exquisite tablecloth from the bag. It was white with arranged floral decorations. It was beautiful, unique, and wrapped in a thick cloth bag like an old treasure. She told me that her grandmother had made it. Nonno Suiko began to weave its yarn when Maria was born. She kept weaving it for five whole years. It was said that her grandmother did not surrender to death until the day after she was sure that the last node was finished. She declared in her will that the family should keep this tablecloth until the day Maria moved to her husband's home. On that day, it would be the wedding gift offered to her granddaughter from the other world.

I trembled when my fingers touched the fine needlework; it was as if I were shaking hands with old, kind fingers. I contemplated all the effort and years an old lady from another age took just to add a beautiful touch to the house of a man she would never know.

I felt that the fabric was haunted by the spirit of love which could be transmitted through time, just as genes, features, and eye colour can be transmitted.

I noticed that Maria was praying for her grandmother. I read some Quran verses for her and asked God to have mercy on her. Our prayers were united, then our hands, then our lips, then our bodies, as if it was a united prayer with different languages praying for God the merciful Creator, who created love in our hearts, to bypass time, distance, colour, tongue, and speech.

. . . . .

The Seventh Voyage

The Mediterranean Sea, 1269

With fear and hope, the ship sailed the sea.

I asked Youness the Egyptian about the story of the cardinal and why the papal chair was left empty. Why were the Franks not able to inaugurate a pope as they were hundreds of years ago? He stared into the distance as if talking to a ghost standing in between the horizon and the sea, and started to talk.

"Since the holy words were bought and sold and Simony became the religion of those who were sitting in the Holy Temple, the silver of Simon the Magician had the upper hand over the reign of Saint Peter the Apostle. Then the iron of the swords had the upper hand above all. The necks and hearts bowed down to the will of the thrones and the sceptre; the sons of the Kingdom of Heaven obeyed the will of the kings of thorns. Kings had conflicting desires. Each wanted the one who would be the pope to be loyal to his throne; thus, everything failed. Two great thrones in Europe are now fighting over it. On one hand, there is the king of the Germans, who extended his influence and authority to the island of Cyprus and the Temple Knights. On the other hand, there is the king of the Franks, your uncle, who is now preparing for a new crusade against Western Tunisia after being defeated twenty years ago in Egypt and Mansoura. A few months ago, there were battles between both thrones near Rome. Victory was exchanged until the final moment, when your uncle conquered Conardine, the young king of the Germans, and executed him. Now the Temple Knights want to respond with another victory; if the Franks king won the war, then he would be able to win the papal chair. When their cardinal becomes pope, it will be a glorious victory and eloquent response to the defeat of the swords and knights."

I was touched by Youness talking about my uncle, as if he spoke to remind me of the main reason for my trip. The royal blood running in my veins calls me from beyond the sea and sunset. My mother's weak voice comes from an unknown grave that was trampled by the horses of Al Tatar outside the city of Homs. The noble tattoo is carved with fire on my arms, and the dragon blows flame in the golden ring. The threads of the journey of life intersect with the cycles of days... the spirits are held by God's hand and His will.

I asked Youness about my expected meeting with my father. Before I started the journey, I believed that once my father saw me, he would know that his blood is in my veins. A long past memory of falling in love with a woman under the shadow of swords would resurface. Our hearts would beat together, although he would probably become confused because of the presence of the priests, the court men, and the tough knights. But then he would honour my arrival, despite the astonishment. Secretly, he would be yearning to ask me about the memory of his beloved woman. He would check all the details of my face, my nose, my chin, and my forehead, searching for the features of the captive woman who was proud of her dignity and honour. Before I started the journey, I told this story to myself hundreds of times with different details, but I never took into consideration the fear of denial, the risk of competition with the heirs of the royal blood, or the accusation of pretense and abuse of noble descent.

Before I started the journey, the thorny details did not fill my path; but after I tried the bitterness of captivity and the dangers of travelling, I realized that fulfilling my mother's covenant was fraught with immeasurable risks. My ultimate hope was to be in the crowd lined up to greet my father and uncle in the seasonal celebration. I would stare into his eyes from afar; I would find some of the blueness of my eyes; or I would break through the crowds and touch the hem of his robe, like patients who await the healing touch of their king.

Youness looked at me tenderly, and his deep soul leaked from his two open eyes as he said, "You might have a chance in Rome. Your Frank uncle is now mobilizing cavalry and nobility to carry out his new crusade. Your father, the prince, always travels with him. Yes, your chance is in Rome. If the new pope is inaugurated, most likely King Louis IX will go to receive his blessing. Rome is filled with strangers, pilgrims, adventurers, and seekers of forgiveness. It would be easier to mingle with them and get closer to the king among them, rather than go to the capital and break into the court, which is forbidden for the common people and the mob."

"Do you really believe that kings have a healing touch? I heard that people infected with the Pig's Disease[15] wait for weeks at the gates of the King of Franks for the king to have pity on them and provide them with his healing touch… I can mingle with these crowds waiting to meet my father."

I did not tell Youness the Egyptian that since I heard this story, I believed that my talent for treatment comes from the royal blood in my veins and not because of my knowledge of veterinary sciences and aromatherapy. Is it the son of the veterinarian Al Bitar or the Son of Prince Pitar who treats the patients? The

---

[15] Its scientific name is scrofula, a disease in the neck's lymph nodes that make the infected person look like he has the neck of a pig. Pig's Disease was known in the Middle Ages as King's Evil because of the belief that the touch of kings could heal it.

question puzzled me while I was curing the sick, suffering sailors on the ship and my partners in slavery on Cyprus Island.

Youness the Egyptian read the question in my eyes and answered:

"Son, kings have their own circumstances. God created healing in the hearts and not in the royal blood. Have you ever heard about Saint Verena, the Egyptian virgin who taught the pagan Europeans how to treat their diseases and cleanse their bodies from the causes of the disease? Verena was not a descendant of a royal family, but God gave her the healing touch and science of herbs like you, my son."

It was clear that I did not understand, thus Youness continued to narrate a story that had been written on papyrus for centuries, until it reached him:

"This took place during the era of the Roman Pagan King Diocletian who came to Egypt. The people of Egypt hosted him generously and honoured him with a famous monument which is still standing in the city of Alexandria. The Diocletian Army was engaged in a fierce war in Gaul, which became the land of the Franks. He wanted to reinforce his army with the Egyptian Copts, so he gathered over six thousand young men to join his army and called them the *Theban Battalion*, meaning *The Egyptian Group*. The Egyptians showed great courage in fighting the enemies of the king until he won the war. Diocletian gave orders to hold celebrations, declaring that the soldiers should burn incense for his statue, since he was the victorious god king. But the Copts of the Theban Battalion refused to worship the king or burn incense for him, for they believed in only one God. The king became angry and gave orders that The Theban Battalion stand in lines for the gladiator to pass before them and whip then behead one out of ten soldiers. But rather than encouraging them to recant, the others became even more staunch in their faith. In the end, the king had to kill all of them because none of the Copts recanted. This happened in the third year of the Martyrs."

I listened and wondered. This story reminded me of the Jihad of the early companions of Prophet Mohamed at the beginning of the appearance of Islam in Mecca and the torture by the Tatar of the people of Levant that I witnessed during my childhood. It seems that winning hearts is a recurrent desire of everyone who has had authority or power over the ages. The sword has one religion, and the king's religion is the same no matter how different the beliefs or the religions.

"But how is this related to the Saint Verena you told me about?" I asked.

"Verena, my son, was one of the Coptic maidens that accompanied the battalion to prepare food and cure the injured. She was from Gargos, a town near Thebes in Upper Egypt. Her name means 'the good fruit' in Coptic. Although she witnessed the massacre of her people, she escaped and fled to foreign lands. Living in a cave, she started to teach the pagan Franks about hygiene and medical treatment with herbs. She faced abuse with love; thus, God gave her a healing touch. She was the reason why the army of Diocletian and the Franks believed in God. Love, my child, heals the hearts. Love defeats the sword. And the blood of the martyrs defeated the arrogance of kings."[16]

I was unable to respond as the Genoese captain stormed up to us at that moment. With anger marring his features, he pointed to Youness the Egyptian, while Hassan tried to calm him, screaming:

"An escaped slave! If the Hospitallers' ships catch us, it will be our end; they would never hesitate to pursue those fleeing their island!"

---

[16] Some historians believe that the Egyptian Saint Verena is the mother of nuns in Europe. She died in 344 AD and a church was built where she was buried in the city of Tembortach in Switzerland. There are seventy churches in Switzerland and thirty churches in Germany that carry her name. The statues and icons usually represent her as a woman with a water jar and a comb in her hand.

"The Cypriots will not realize that Youness escaped until later. They are unlikely to link his flight with the departure of our ship. They might believe that another beast came and ate him," Hassan replied.

"Are you joking, Hassan? Do you not realize that the eyes of the Hospitallers are in every port? Did you not know that the cardinal has sent ambassadors to all the harbours of Europe announcing the miracle achieved by him? You are witnesses and participated in the incident; it is important for the cardinal that it be told exactly the way he wants! Any undesirable details can be considered by the cardinal as blasphemous and sowing skepticism about the miracle, which he would never allow. You are putting yourselves in danger, and I do not want to be a part of this. I have fulfilled my promise and paid my debt to you and your sheikh."

The final sentence uttered by the Genoa captain to Hassan drew my attention. But now was not the time to ask about it. The captain stormed off, Hassan in tow. When Hassan came back to us, he was very worried. He told us that the captain had decided to leave Youness the Egyptian on the Italian coast, as he did not want to bear the responsibility of having an escaping slave on board his ship while the Cypriot ships fill the sea like hungry wolves.

When I told Hassan that I would accompany Youness to his destiny, he smiled and said that he expected that. He had agreed with the captain to leave the three of us on the Amalfi coast in Italy. From there, we would continue our trip to Rome. This worked out quite well, as Amalfi was closer to Rome than Genoa. In Rome, all roads converge, and people meet from all over the Earth. We would inevitably find a way to return to our country.

A hot tear escaped the eyes of Youness. It rebelled against the prison of his eyelids and went down to disappear into his long white beard. He told me that all he wanted was to die in Egypt, but he would accompany me to Rome to fulfill my promise to my dead mother. A look in the eyes of my father or my uncle would be enough. I would find my features in theirs, and then my mother will be innocent in my eyes forever.

Demotic Hymn for Youness the Egyptian

"AN AGE WAS SPENT ON THE ROAD...
THEN WE REALIZED THAT THE GOAL
WAS THE JOURNEY ITSELF."

Autumn has its Own Journey

Cairo, November 2011

During my childhood and youth, I stood on the beach of Alexandria for long periods of time facing the September breeze, which reduced the heat of the summer and emptied the beach of holidaymakers and their noise. I would raise my eyes to watch the birds coming in from the horizon. I would watch them seemingly hanging in space aligned in a wonderful system, as if they were racing the next winter clouds which were coming from somewhere beyond.

Al Saleeb Winds, western winds that rarely bring rain, come into the city at the end of September to mark the beginning of the winter seasonal storms in Alexandria. These winds are the first thing that sweeps the heat of the summer out and reminds us of the beginning of autumn. These winds come with a touch of cold and quail birds, urging mothers to get out the long-sleeved shirts and light pullovers from the clothing cabinets that are filled with naphthalene. Blankets are thrown over beds and rebellious kids and teenagers don't listen to their mother's advice to wear a jacket at night. When the Al Maknasa storm comes, it means that winter has arrived.

Everything has its time. Every trip has its cycle. It is stupid to ask where the spring travels when it is chased by other seasons.

From the plane, I was trying hard to see through the clouds, searching for the point where we passed the coast. I might be able to see my city which the quail birds had crossed during the past weeks. The pilot asked us to fasten our seat belts and get ready for landing. I realized that my Alexandria had passed, that it was Cairo below that coming cluster of fog.

This was the first time Maria and I had been apart since we met. I was the one who had gotten used to travelling a lot, but it was the first time in a long time that I experienced the storm of tears at the airport. I could not hold myself together when she hugged me, crying, and put her small head on my chest. She asked me several times if she could accompany me on this trip but I refused. I was afraid of the rumour that my name was on the arrival checklists, despite the confirmation from my father's friends that this was not true and that there was no judicial order issued to arrest me as reported in forums on the internet, citing The Believers Channel. I was afraid that my father's friends had the wrong information and that I would exit the airport handcuffed, leaving Maria confused and puzzled in a strange land she knew very little about.

Events had escalated unexpectedly and strangely during the past weeks.

I became focused on establishing my new life. Work on the Ibn Al Bitar cache was on hold, waiting for the cumbersome restoration process. I started my work at La Sapienza University, and was swept into administrative and academic preparations for the next school year. I flew with Maria in the sky of happiness. We began to furnish an apartment worthy of our love which crossed the times and distances and also one worthy of her grandmother's antique tablecloth. We planned for our upcoming life with details including the wedding, the honeymoon trip, and the names of our children who would have blue eyes and Japanese features, challenging the boundaries between human features.

The news coming from Egypt was filled with more bloodshed, clashes, and massacres.

The military junta, allied with Islamists and extremists, drove thousands of terrorists out of prison and issued a general amnesty that brought thousands of al-Qaeda and jihadist organizations back from distant fighting places in Afghanistan, Iraq and elsewhere, pushing them to clash with the liberal and civil currents that revolutionized.

The military rulers committed a massacre in October 2011 against Christian demonstrators[17] in front of the television building. The demonstrators were demanding freedom to build churches; dozens of them were killed. The army tanks literally crushed the bodies of the demonstrators, but Islamist television channels defended the killers. The authorities then arrested political activists who demonstrated in protest against the massacre.

The former terrorists had been active in beating and destroying all those who demand the principles of freedom and democracy for which the revolution was founded.

A fight in Al Abbasiya Square, a massacre in Mohamed Mahmoud Street, the sit-ins in Tahrir Square, with everyone wanting to take advantage, claiming ownership of the slogans of the revolution… Military people, bearded men, youth, revolutionaries, old regime loyalists, and others played on the ropes of the slogans.

Everyone was rallying for hastily held elections under the influence of the military and the Islamists.

I became unable to understand. I could not continue, for I was exhausted by the mixed information and tangled threads. The distance between Rome and Cairo diverged until I woke one morning to an Egyptian number on the screen of my mobile. The insistent ringing urged me to answer the phone though I was not completely

---

[17] This event, known as the Maspiro massacre, took place on 9th October, 2011.

awake. A rough voice asked me if I was Professor Daniel Abd El Razak. After confirming that I was, he yelled at me, "Damn you and your fellow dirty Copts of the diaspora! You will burn in Hell! You are not far from our hands; the swords of Islam will cut off your head very soon!"

It took me time to fully wake up and understand what had happened, although I did not understand what he had said. During the next few days, I started following again what was happening in Egypt. I was shocked to find out that my name was one of those mentioned in the media. The Believers Channel considered me a target to be attacked. People were discussing on internet forums my alleged role in the Copts of the diaspora. Rumours varied: some said that my father, the apostate, baptized me when I was a small child; while others considered me a convert. But all agreed that I was hostile toward Islam and Muslims and that I diligently and persistently worked to tarnish the image of religion in the West.

Maria said this was because I did not defend myself from the beginning when rumours first starting spreading that I was a convert and that I joined the so-called Copts of the diaspora, but I had felt that it was ridiculous to defend myself against this kind of accusation.

"What did you want me to do, call the talk show programs to defend my religion and convince them that I am Muslim? To record a video of myself praying and upload it on YouTube? The humiliation I felt last time I had the call with the famous presenter to defend my father's religion was enough. I lived in Britain for years while preparing my PhD thesis at Cambridge University. I saw there that just asking about anyone's religion was prohibited. I remember an Indian colleague sued one of the British professors only because he asked him about his religion. This Indian colleague considered the question itself unlawful discrimination. It was only because of the great efforts made by the university to contain the situation and satisfy the Indian colleague that the British professor was not exposed to serious legal consequences. But this did not prevent the

British professor from quitting, and this incident chased him for a long time after that."

"My love, you are talking about a different society. European societies suffered for decades from discrimination and religious war. They lived during a time when the Catholics were burned just because they lived in a Protestant country — and vice versa. The Holocaust is not an ancient European history but a contemporary tragedy. Religious, sectarianism, and ethnic fanaticism have smashed Western societies; that's why they deal with these issues with extreme sensitivity and impose strict and decisive laws to avoid repeating them. The Western world knows that racism and intolerance are an integral part of their heritage; they are aware that they are forced to rebel against this inheritance and heritage after centuries and centuries of violence and bloodshed."

Maria's broken voice reflected the weight of her personal experience. The colour of her skin and her eyes were prisons surrounding her in the twenty-first century as they once surrounded her grandmother in American concentration camps in the 1940s. Maria never told me about the racial harassment or discrimination in Italy because of the colour of her skin and the shape of her eyes. People dealt with her different features as something interesting rather than something embarrassing or painful, perhaps because the feelings of racism in Italy were mainly directed at African migrants, Moroccans and Arabs who flocked to the peninsula, changing its population structure, putting pressure on the labour market and jobs, thus provoking racist hostility… Or possibly because the Italians were so used to directing their racism against other Europeans, especially the Franks, they no longer had enough hatred for an Italian girl with Japanese features.

Maria had asked me before to deal with the rumours, to contact Egyptian media and declare to them that I did not join the Copts of the Diaspora. But she was still deeply annoyed by my sudden decision to travel to Cairo. She begged me not to travel. She wanted me to just call the talk show or issue a statement to send to journalists and writers who were friends of my father. But I felt deep inside that this was not enough. This time, rumours were not insulting me and my father. They were specific. Social media sites were displaying scenes from a film that attacked the Prophet Mohamed. In Egypt, people were saying that a group of Copts of the diaspora produced that film, and that I participated in funding it, and that I even represented the role of the prophet in the film.

I did not know what brought my name into this ridiculous issue, but the rumours had gone too far. I received dozens of phone calls daily, some of them threatening and insulting me, others from the friends of my father sympathizing with me, but for some unknown reason, showing some hidden blame. Maybe this case cast shame on the memory of my father and the political party he represented. Certainly, these rumours affected all the symbols of his party amid the hysterical political conflicts in Egypt.

A few days prior, Tariq Mamdouh, the programmer of the famous talk show program, called me, inviting me to be a guest on the program where I could deny this accusation. I thought about it a little bit and told him I did not want it to be a phone call like the last time. I wanted to be in the studio and discuss this silly accusation. I wanted to prove that I was not guilty and that my name was not on the arrival checklist. This time, I would face the rumours; I would not bury them in a cycle of work and love as I had done before.

Once the plane landed in Cairo, I got out my mobile phone. I called my father's friend, the famous journalist, keeping the line open while I went through customs. He was confident that my name was not on the arrival checklist and that there were no real accusations against me unlike what the rumours said. But he was also afraid I might face some unexpected harassment or unusual procedures.

"Being with you over the phone will let me know immediately if you are arrested or if they take your passport, and I will know what to do to save you. But note that the first thing they ask you to do is to turn off your mobile phone and give it to them."

Leaving the airport did not take a long time. My small bag which I always carry helped me again to avoid the crowded luggage line. A few minutes later, I was on a taxi heading to a hotel in the 6th of October neighbourhood. I will be a few steps away from the studio of the famous talk show program where I was scheduled to appear that night.

I called Maria to let her know that I was safe. I tried to wipe her tears away with some jokes promising her that I would be back in two days. I could not be in Egypt without visiting Alexandria, so I would travel to Rome directly from Al Nozha International Airport in Alexandria.

The traffic jam in Cairo was unbearable. Chaos lay in the black streets and grey pavements. Human footsteps were mixed with turning tires, and angry yelling blended with the roaring of the engines. I saw anger on the faces and features that could seemingly explode with the slightest provocation. Autumn was all over the sky with clouds full of car exhaust. The driver exhaled deeply while complaining of the circumstances. He heard me talking over the phone in English and Italian, so he started talking about Western civilization and how the streets were clean, organized, and managed properly, contrary to what was happening in Cairo.

"That's why, although they are infidels, God honours them. You know, sir, when Begin of Israel visited Egypt for the Peace Treaty, he said that as long as the streets of Cairo are full of chaos, there is no fear for our state. I would worry for Israel if the Egyptians learned to stand in a queue in an organized way."

I remembered an article I had read a few days prior in one of the Egyptian newspapers. The writer said that the sharp polarizing situation in Egyptian society was reflected by taxi drivers. They were the segment of the population that faced the reality of everyday life with its bitterness, the chaos of the streets, and the polemic discussions that took place among people. The drivers instinctively realized the persuasion of the occupant and tried to say what he wanted to hear. They did not want to have a conflict with the client, who was going to pay for the ride at the end and might add a tip according to the skillful driver and his ability to say what the passenger liked to hear. Thus, those who read the blogs of political activists who were pro-revolution and their discussions with the taxi drivers would think that all the drivers were pro-revolution, just as those who read the blogs of those who were supporting the old regime would think that all the drivers yearned for Mubarak.

I tried to test this theory with the driver who exhaled deeply and stuck his head outside the window from time to time to yell or curse at one of the other drivers or the pedestrians. I asked him about the conditions of the country; he started criticizing everything. I might have regretted asking this question because it took us two and a half hours to arrive at the hotel, and he did not stop talking the entire time. I heard all the political, economic, and sociological theories mixed with insults and curses for all the existing and previous political parties, with faith placed in only two: the army and the sheikhs of religion who sought to reform society and apply God's law. At the end of the ride, when he felt satisfied with the tip I gave him, he summarized his wisdom in a few words:

"Look, sir, we are a nation who has gotten used to taking orders. Listening and obeying are the basics of both the army and religion. That's why we should only be governed by one of them."

That evening, about an hour before the program, Tariq Mamdouh called me to ensure that I had arrived and to inform me that a car would pick me up from the hotel in fifteen minutes to take me to the studio.

"No need for the car. The hotel is steps away from the media production neighbourhood. I prefer to walk to the studio. I might even arrive before the car."

I said the last sentence with a sense of humour, but Tariq replied in a serious and decisive tone:

"No, Professor, I prefer that you ride in the car. The driver has the necessary permit to enter the media production neighbourhood but also…"

He paused and seemed to hesitate for a moment before completing his sentence:

"Also, there are protestors standing in front of the gate. They tried to enter the studio but security stopped them. I am afraid that some of them might harass you on sight."

"Protestors? Why? What are they protesting?"

"Unfortunately, the Believers Channel is launching a severe campaign against you, turning people against you. I do not know how they found out that you are going to be a guest on the program tonight, but when they did, Sheikh Hatem Kamal El Din called his followers to besiege the compound and prevent you from entering."

He paused again for a few seconds as if waiting for my comment, only to continue, after I remained silent:

"Anyway, do not worry, Professor Daniel… besieging the city with demonstrations by bearded men is something normal now. It is worth being cautious about, but it does not deserve worrying. There is nothing to be afraid of."

I hung up the phone and got ready. The clouds in the sky foreshadowed a cold night; I wondered if I should take my coat since I might get out of the studio pretty late at night. When reception informed me that the driver was waiting for me, I was ready to leave.

I could see the gate of the media production compound from the gate of the hotel and I could hear the chanting led by a small microphone saying:

> "Here we are, Heroic Islam, to protect all that should be protected."

I sat in the back seat as the driver said, so that I was not visible to anyone outside thanks to blackened windows. When the car drew close to the gate of the media production compound, I noticed that the crowd was much smaller than I had expected. There were fewer than twenty people, but the microphones they were using increased the impact of their voices. Their enthusiasm, the way they moved, and their organized collective cheering also augmented the effect of their presence.

When the car came closer, I became worried as we would soon be passing through the crowd. I read some of the signs they were raising: 'I would sacrifice my mother and father for you, my beloved prophet,' 'O God, burn those who harm our Islam.' Some signs were written in English, too, saying: 'USA STOP THE BULLSHIT.' I read the sign out loud, and I could not prevent myself from smiling. It seemed that the driver saw me in the mirror, so he warned me not to show anything that the protestors would view as me ridiculing them or their signs.

Some of the protestors were armed with sticks and bricks and were checking the cars entering the compound as if searching them, waving the sticks in front of the car in a challenging manner, raising their voices while cheering. Some of them leaned toward the front glass of the car, checking the faces of the driver and the passengers. Going through the crowds did not take a long time, probably less than a minute, but I was so nervous waiting that it felt like much longer. The huge iron gate guarded by a police car with red and blue colours glowing above it appeared before us. I looked at the police car. A young officer sitting in the front seat holding a wireless transmitter caught my eye. We greeted each other with a faint smile. I breathed a sigh of relief as the guards stopped the car, asking the driver for his permit.

What happened in the next few seconds took me by complete surprise.

Everything transpired so quickly.

I heard something hit the back of the car. When I turned to look, the blood froze in my veins. The crowd was running and throwing bricks at the car. Cracks appeared in the glass; I could not see through it anymore. I turned to look in front of me; I noticed the young officer still sitting holding the wireless transmitter, the blue and red lights still throbbing silently. The front of the car was stuck by the iron gate which had not yet been opened by the guards. The angry crowd reached the car and started hitting the windows with the sticks while screaming violently, thirsty for blood.

Before darkness prevailed…the blue and red lights were stained with dark spots… and a hot sticky liquid filled my mouth with the taste of salt and gunpowder...

"O PEOPLE, KNOW THAT GOD HAS ALLOWED
YOU TO SHED MY BLOOD,
KILL ME YOU WILL RECOMPENSE
AND I WILL BE RELIEVED,
KILL ME AND YOU WILL BE CONSIDERED BY
GOD AS FIGHTERS AND I WILL BE CONSIDERED
A MARTYR."

THE PHILOSOPHER ABOU EL MOGHEITH AL
HUSSEIN IBN MANSOUR AL HALAG
(EXECUTED IN 922)

The Final Voyage

Darkness covers everything. And yet, it is fragile; you can feel it, almost. You can almost touch it just by stretching your hand.

Darkness deactivates the eyes but activates other senses. You hear whispers, footsteps, the swish of a dress. You hear spirits floating in the air you are breathing.

I tasted the sharpness of the salty blood which filled my mouth. I felt like the ground was cotton. I felt the smile of my father somewhere close by.

My hand was still touching the emptiness. It went to my face but did not find it. Instead of my eyes, there was a wide hole that led nowhere.

The whispers continued, turning into words tinged with fear and silent pauses filled with caution and anticipation.

> **"We have to separate. The cardinal's knights are looking for three people. We will have a better chance if each one of us mingles alone with the crowd."**

I knew this voice without having heard it before. It combined dignity with wisdom. It belonged to someone with a long white beard.

"Hassan rushed. He cut the ear of the soldier who stopped us at the gates of the city with his pointed dagger. We could have passed among the crowd without being revealed had he not done that."

"What should I have done? The soldier wanted to go through our luggage. He would have certainly found your damn papers. People here are killed for carrying things like papers written in foreign language. They will consider it a magical spell and sentence to death the one carrying it."

"We have to bury it, then, somewhere safe in the woods."

"We might have to stay outside Rome… Entering the city is risky. The soldiers are guarding the entrances and there aren't many places we can hide. But the countryside is vast and has larger areas suitable for hiding."

"On the contrary. All the strangers in the area enter the city, but the presence of strangers in the countryside would be suspicious as none go there. When the holidays are over and the crowds are gone, we can mingle with the strangers returning home without raising any doubts."

I felt a painful sting in the crook of my arm, yet my heartbeat's pulse was somewhere outside my body. The blue and red lights were still flickering on and off. The officer's wireless transmitter emitted an audible rattle and then a meaningless whistle. I opened my mouth but my voice wouldn't come out. I heard someone calling for the one who held the pointed dagger.

"Before the sun turns two complete rounds, one of you will be crucified on the cross of the city. God will choose which one."

My voice went hoarse, creating a moment of silence filled with tension... were people listening to my words? I did not know... But the dignified voice returned in the deep dark, saying:

> "We will bury our papers here. We might come back later to get the papyrus out, if we survive. I did not want you to be tormented with the fear of anticipation and pursuit because of me, but it is our destiny. I know that the cardinal knows that we are undesired witnesses of his story. He wants to remove our tongues, so we can't say what he does not want anyone to know. People in Rome are gathering to meet him; they are cheering for the saviour whose faith defeated the dragon of the last days."
>
> "He might be the Antichrist. People will be so impressed by him that they will obey him without seeing the word *liar* written on his forehead. My sheikh and teacher was right. It is time for Mawlay Al Mahdi, who will inevitably come to fill the world with justice after being filled with injustice and oppression."
>
> The fugitives share water.

How incredibly thirsty I am.

> They get out some dry bread and dates, and, as they complete their last supper, a vow is made.
>
> "If the soldiers catch either of us, he should tell them that the other two died during the journey. Even if he is tortured and his flesh is torn with iron claws, he has to keep the secret of his two companions so that he may be a sacrifice to save the other two."

The vow echoed in the dark… carrying the different names of the one God… Multiple tributaries flowed into the Great River, the creator of life on both banks… granting human beings, animals, plants, houses, and roads the secret of permanence… The greatness of the river lay in the multiplicity of its tributaries… In the ether cloud around us, a voice echoed and the universe listened:

> *"O you with the pointed dagger*
> *Split people's hearts*
> *You won't find anything*
> *But blood*
> *Split the heart of the traitor, the ugly, the thief, and the Malicious*
> *In the hearts of the kind people*
> *You won't find anything*
> *But blood*
> *All hearts are the same under the tip of the daggers*
> *Iron does not open hearts*
> *But rather it tears them apart*
> *Only light touches the buds of the hearts, thus it blossoms*
> *Verena the good seed*
> *Conquered the Roman swords with love*
> *Cured the hearts of the murderers with forgiveness*
> *With the healing touch*
> *O you, with the pointed dagger*
> *God created life*
> *Prohibited murder*
> *Cursed the murderer*
> *But God's religion is violated by those representing it*
> *Those who were murdered by the name of God,*
> *Are double or even more than those who were murdered in the name of Satan"*

. . . . .

"Thank God, he is opening his eyes! Daniel? Daniel?"

I heard the voice in the darkness. I saw Maria's glow seeping through, lighting up my heart even as my eyes remained shut. I heard my voice as if it were coming from a deep abysmal cave.

"Maria!"

The scent of her hair was the first thing that made me realize that I was still alive. Her soft face, a sharp contrast to the roughness of my stubble, touched my cheek as she kissed me.

I tried to move, but my hands were restricted. Were they tied? Surely, I had not been that bad a patient, trying to pull the tubing connecting my body to the fluids that would help heal it.

I felt like I was still floating in endless darkness. Someone asked me, in English with a heavy German accent, how I was doing. I posed endless questions which Maria answered patiently, albeit with an underlying anxiety:

> "We are in Berlin. Professor Wolfgang Chtayen is personally supervising your treatment. You were in a coma for a week in Cairo, until the doctors advised us to take you to Berlin for specialized care. The critical phase passed two weeks ago. The doctors are confident that your body will respond to therapy and that it is just a matter of time until you are fully recovered."

> "My eyes... Is there a bandage on them?"

> "Temporarily, sweetheart. You will gradually regain your eyesight."

Her voice was quavering a bit, and I felt her hand touching my cheek. It had been too much for me, it seemed, and I could feel darkness engulfing me again. It was going to be like this for some time. As I went from one operation to another, I would spend large amounts of time sleeping and recuperating.

Throughout it all, Maria was there with me, reminding me that there is light everywhere despite the despair, the pain, and the nightmares of darkness.

Somewhere in the unknown world lay a child with blue eyes and Japanese features, waiting for the moment he could come to life.

The End

www.ingramcontent.com/pod-product-compliance
Lightning Source LLC
LaVergne TN
LVHW041636060526
838200LV00040B/1600